Daughters of the Blue Moon

Millie Abecassis

Anuci Press

Tanuci69@gmail.com

First paperback edition 2025

Anuci Press edition 2025

www.anuci-press.com

Cover Design by Ruth Anna Evans

ruthannaevans.com (google.com)

Edited by Katarina Yerger

ISBN 979-8-9919612-1-9 (paperback)

ISBN 979-8-9919612-2-6 (eBook)

Contents

Chapter One

Now

The shepherd found the first dead ewe lying on its side, the belly wide open and what remained of its entrails crudely spread around it. Surprisingly, its wool was gone, too. No beast could shear a sheep, so the villagers first suspected that some*one* had killed it. But the bite marks on the ewe's belly were the herald of a wolf—or a vicious dog, perhaps. A villager suggested that a deranged man had ordered his companion to attack and kill the ewe so he could steal the wool and meat. Then he had let his dog feast on the corpse once his disgraceful work was over. That, or the culprit was indeed a wolf, another villager offered, and some poor lad had found the dead animal before dawn. Instead of warning the shepherd, he must have seized the opportunity to make himself some warm clothing before the winter. The latter theory sounded far-fetched to everyone, and to the shepherd most of all. The sun had barely risen when he had found his animal dead in a pool of blood. The kill was fresh, so fresh that he had shivered, looking around him to check the murderer wasn't around anymore. Whoever had sheared the ewe must have also killed and gutted it, he knew.

His conviction was put to the test only two weeks later, when he found another dead ewe roughly hidden in the long grass of his pasture. This time its wool was intact, except for the parts that had covered the skin around its throat and vital organs. Its body, like the first ewe, was still in one piece. If this was the work of a wolf—and it certainly was, the shepherd thought—then it was a lone one. A pack would have torn the ewe apart. He had seen it happen before the village's hunters killed most of the wolves haunting the woods around Ozaryn. The last survivors of the pack had either starved or fled. But the shepherd wondered: what if one had come back and was hungry for the flesh of his gentle animals, much easier targets than the fierce deer roaming the forest?

When he found the third body, savagely devoured as if the wolf had not eaten for months, Ozaryn's villagers agreed to help him pay for a hunter's services. They naturally turned to Carmine and Dacien, the best hunters in the region. Carmine and Dacien usually hunted together, for Dacien had trained Carmine himself before marrying her, but a more important hunt had called him to another town, and Carmine agreed to take on the hunt by herself—but not without her husband's blessing.

Hunting alone didn't scare Carmine. She had more than her husband's blessing to protect her from the wolves: her training, her bow, her knives, and her grandmother's spell, forever embedded into her skin. Expanding from her shoulders to her lower back, the magical tattoo spiraled in an intricate pattern reminiscent of lightning, its still-vivid black ink protecting her against a predator that had, once upon a time, almost killed her. Now she didn't fear wolves anymore. She would make quick work of that sheep-killer. She tracked it from the pasture, following the bloody trail, then the unmistakable wolf tracks that led her to a wolf's den.

The den was empty. Good. The spell prevented wolves from smelling Carmine, allowing her to plan deadly ambushes. She carefully set a steel-jaw trap and hid it under a bed of orange leaves. Then, glancing around, she searched for the best place to hide to have a clear shot. She had to act fast, as she couldn't foretell when the wolf would come back. No magic could see the future, not even her grandmother's powerful witchcraft. She found a tree easy enough to climb up, and perched on one of its highest branches, ready to shoot.

It'd better come soon, she thought. The prospect of spending the night perched in a tree didn't appeal to her. Wolves may not scare her anymore, but the night brought other dangers, the cold being the most lethal of them.

The sun was low on the horizon when a lean, four-legged silhouette detached itself from the trees. A male, adolescent, but already strong like an adult, Carmine assessed. She wouldn't risk fighting it alone in close combat. Its jaws could snap her neck in a second, and even if her grandmother's spell protected her, she wouldn't test it. The magic was strong, but the more wolves challenged it, the more likely it could fail. Her grandmother had reminded her so many times: *Don't tempt fate.* But no wolf could threaten her with a paw stuck inside merciless steel and an arrow lodged inside its chest. Carmine held her breath, waiting for the sheep-killer to step into the bed of dead leaves, her bow drawn and ready to send a fixed-blade broadhead inside her victim's heart.

The wolf stopped moving. It had sensed something. But what? She had been careful. It couldn't smell her, and the tree hid her well. Could it be the leaves? Had she failed, in her haste, to make it look natural? All she needed was for the wolf to take one more step, and it would trigger the trap. But it didn't, and instead, it lowered its head and sniffed the leaves before slowly taking a step back.

Carmine only had a second to choose: let the wolf leave and come back tomorrow with a better plan, or engage it and pray for her first arrow to find the beast's heart. She didn't hesitate and released the arrow. If she gave up now and tried again the next day, Dacien would accompany her, as he was expected to come back from his own hunt by dawn. Some villagers believed women weren't fit for solo hunts—or hunting, period—and she wanted to prove them wrong. The arrow ripped through the air and lodged itself inside the wolf's chest, who yelped before falling to the side. It let out a deep, low growl before falling silent, its dead eyes staring into the void. She had made a perfect shot.

Carmine climbed down the tree and approached the fresh carcass. She kneeled down, ready to take the arrow out, when the wolf suddenly raised its head and opened its mouth to attempt to sink its fangs inside her neck. Carmine rolled to her side, half-instinctively, half-pushed by her spell's magic. The wolf's jaws snapped shut in the air only a few inches from her, and she didn't wait for it to try biting again to draw a hunting knife and stab the beast in the neck. It yelped again, louder than the first time, until the cry died in its throat as it choked on its own blood. The stillness of death seized the wolf's body, its face forever caught in a silent agony. The yellow eyes that were filled with anger only seconds ago now stared lifelessly at Carmine, giving the fierce animal the appearance of a harmless, fragile doll.

Carmine took a moment to collect herself, slowly understanding what had just happened. The arrow had actually missed the heart, but instead of fleeing, the wolf had played dead, waiting for Carmine to approach so it could try killing her. She had never, ever seen a wolf play dead. Run away or attack when cornered and desperate, yes, but fake death to launch a surprise attack? Something was deeply wrong with this wolf. A good thing that she killed it. Nobody in the village wanted a wickedly astute wolf lurking in the forest and killing their sheep. Perhaps the wolf had belonged to a druid once, before straying from its master. Only a druid could enchant an animal with improved senses, but they kept their animals close to them and would never let them spread terror. And there was no druid in the forest around Ozaryn. No witch either, since Carmine's grandmother had passed away two winters ago. That clever wolf must have come from afar, perhaps running away from the druid who had tamed it originally. Carmine let out a long, shaky breath. Now that the wolf was dead, it didn't matter anymore. She had successfully completed her contract, and it was time to bring the carcass back to the village so she could receive the payment she was owed.

Carefully, Carmine removed the arrow from the wolf's chest. Blood had already soaked parts of the beast's fur. The damage was still minimal, and she had good hopes to sell the fur to one of the traders who regularly visited Ozaryn. Once the arrow was back in its quiver, the knife in its sheath, and the unused trap disarmed and back in its bag, she lifted the wolf and put its body over her shoulder, where a light metal plate covered the leather of her jacket. It was heavy, but not as heavy as a full-grown adult, and though she knew she would have to take a couple of breaks to catch her breath, she would be back to the village before darkness engulfed the woods.

Carmine started walking toward the village, but she had barely taken ten steps away from the wolf's den when she heard hasty footsteps behind her. She was pushed to the ground as a vicious, angry snarl reached her ears. She dropped the carcass and screamed as sharp claws tore her flesh, piercing through her leather jacket and skin like knives into soft butter. Trembling and injured, she drew her hunting knife again, ready to defend herself. An adult she-wolf that had come out of nowhere was standing before her, baring her teeth and growling.

The spell didn't work was Carmine's first thought, quickly followed by *I'm going to die* as she realized she was too badly hurt to fight eighty pounds of pure muscle and hate. She couldn't see what her back looked like, but the pain told Carmine her injuries were severe. She could bleed out if she didn't get healed soon. For the first time since she began the hunt, Carmine wished Dacien was here to repel the furious beast in front of her. There was a reason hunters preferred to work in pairs, and she was experiencing it in the most brutal, painful way.

"Back off," she said, slashing the knife in front of her while staring at the beast, unblinking. She had no hope of killing the she-wolf, but if she could scare it enough—perhaps injure it, too—that might convince it to retreat. Carmine needed to look strong and not as vulnerable as she actually felt. She rose, stifling the cry of agony that wanted to escape her throat, and repeated, her voice louder, "Back off!"

The she-wolf moved to the side to circle her, but Carmine turned to keep facing it. Her bow was still on her back, but the arrows had flown from their quiver when she had fallen to the ground. Anyway, she was quick, but not quick enough to shoot at a deadly predator only a few feet away from her. The beast would be on her before she could draw her bow. All that stood between her neck and a row of razor-like teeth was her knife and her grit.

Carmine slowly walked backwards, hoping to put some distance between her and the she-wolf, but it lunged at her in a furious growl. She threw herself to the side while slashing at the she-wolf and felt a pang of relief when she heard it yelp in pain. The knife had cut through its right front paw.

"Go away," Carmine said, standing up and leaning forward, making herself as imposing as she could. "I have no quarrel with you." The she-wolf moved to face her again, limping. Carmine slashed the knife in the air again. "Next time, it goes into your neck like that sheep-killer."

The she-wolf stopped growling and curling its lips, and hope to survive the day filled Carmine's chest. She slashed her knife once more, her gaze still fixing the she-wolf's eyes with defiance, before it finally lowered its ears and fled.

Carmine stayed still for a few seconds that felt like hours, waiting for the she-wolf to come back and attack again, but it kept running until it disappeared into the woods. She was safe, at least for now. Every inch of her body shaking, she collected her arrows while gritting her teeth. Every movement felt like torture, and she could feel her blood soaking her jacket where the she-wolf had sunk her claws inside her back. She looked at the sheep-killer's carcass. She couldn't carry it back to the village with what she suspected were deep, life-threatening wounds. No, she had to leave it there and use the last bits of strength she had to get back home before passing out.

Though it normally took only an hour, the walk back to Ozaryn felt like a day-long hike. Carmine couldn't stop looking around for the she-wolf, half expecting it to come back and finish her. She was holding her bow, the nock of an arrow already attached to the string, ready to draw and shoot. Each step felt more painful than the last, but she couldn't slow down. The sun was already below the horizon, its fading light barely providing enough brightness for Carmine to find her way back to the village. As she kept pushing through the forest, she couldn't help but wonder why the spell hadn't protected her against the she-wolf. It had never faltered before. Was the magic becoming unreliable? She had to know if she could count on it or not. Without the magic, she would have to revise her hunting strategy. Be more cautious. Was it because the sheep-killer had attacked her just before, and the magic had been unable to protect her again after so little time had elapsed? If her grandmother were still alive she could ask her, but all she had now to fill the emptiness inside her chest were hypotheses.

A fever had already seized Carmine when she caught a glimpse of Ozaryn's first houses. If it wasn't for Alandra, the shepherd's wife, waiting for her at the edge of the forest, she would have collapsed there and died before dawn. Alandra helped her back into her home before fetching the village's healer. Carmine's house quickly filled up as villagers came to see what had happened. The healer tried to chase them away, saying Carmine needed rest, but the huntress felt the urge to tell them everything. She had killed the wolf responsible for the dead ewes. Her hunt had been successful. She couldn't let them believe she had failed—though she had no proof to sustain her claim, since the carcass was still near the den. She would go retrieve it as soon as possible, she promised, describing where the den was with as much precision as she could, and she would take care of the she-wolf too.

"The men will go retrieve it for you at dawn," Alandra said before Carmine fell into the oblivion of sleep.

The next morning, when Carmine woke up from her slumber, she found her husband seated on the bed next to her, examining her back.

"Did they find the wolf?" she asked. "The sheep-killer."

He slowly shook his head before answering, "They went to the den, but didn't find it."

Chapter Two

Then

The first time Carmine dreamt of wolves, she had just turned fourteen.

It was a vivid dream, so vivid that when she woke up, she remembered the exact shape, color, and smell of the wolves. Their voices too, for she was riding a large gray wolf who talked in a soothing, enchanting voice, while the others sang in harmony. Their song reminded Carmine of the soft whispers of the river flowing through Ozaryn when it rose in the spring, filled with melted snow. A harmony of deep and airy voices filled her ears with a constant rhythm akin to the caress of the water rolling on the rocks of the riverbed. Their song was about the wind brushing their fur and the earth rubbing their paws and the moon flooding their eyes with milky light and the flesh of their prey warming their bellies. Shortly before waking up, she became one with the wolf she had been riding, and sang, too.

She lay in her bed for a long time before getting up. She had never dreamt like this before. The song still resonated in her head, so clearly that she caught herself humming it. Like all the children in Ozaryn, she had learned to be wary of the wild animals living in the forest. Wolves, boars, snakes, and even bears sometimes. But there was something eerily reassuring in the song and in the voices of the wolves, as if they would never hurt her. *We are the sons and daughters of the blue moon,* the song said as it ended, *your brothers and sisters,* leaving Carmine confused by the lyrics' meaning—but wolves wouldn't harm someone they thought of as family, right?

"I dreamt of wolves," she told her parents during breakfast. "Twelve of them, running in the forest and singing a song."

Her mother frowned and glanced at Carmine's father, before saying, "It was just a dream. Eat your porridge now."

Carmine sighed and ate in silence. Her mother had never been affectionate, but it still hurt when she dismissed her like that. As for her father, he had always been kind but distant, as if he couldn't allow himself to love his own daughter as he should.

Her mother had said it was just a dream, but in the evening, Carmine heard her parents quarrel with each other while she was trying to fall asleep—secretly hoping she would dream of wolves again. Her parents never argued. She put her ear on the wall, trying to hear what they were saying, but could only catch snippets of their exchange. Her mother was speaking loudly about bad dreams, while her father was saying that she had said it herself. It was just a dream. The rest was muffled, as if her parents knew she had heard them. Carmine kept listening, hoping to hear more, but the conversation was inaudible until her mother said loudly, "She has bled already!" Carmine removed her ear from the wall and felt her cheeks warm with embarrassment. Had she heard correctly? Had her mother told her father that she just had her first period? Or had she misunderstood? Perhaps she had, or her mother had been talking about something else.

She tried not to think too much about it. Her first period had been painful, and her mother had explained that this would happen every month and meant she could bear children. Carmine didn't want to bear any children. She was still a child herself. Sure, she would soon be seventeen and ready for suitors to propose, but it still sounded so distant, so unreal.

The next morning, Carmine woke up disappointed, not having dreamt of wolves, but she soon forgot about her dreams as her mother prompted her to get ready as quickly as possible.

"Your grandmother is sick," her mother said pressingly, "and the healer wants us to bring her a remedy. Your father needs to craft more shoes for the shop and I'll be busy all day with customers, so I need you to go. Please also take that cake that I just baked."

Carmine stared at her mother. Her grandmother, sick? It had never happened before.

"She's getting older," her mother said, having noticed Carmine's surprise, "and even witches can get colds. It's the season. Go help her. The remedy will make her feel better, and she'll enjoy your company. But stay on the road. Don't take any shortcuts in the forest, you hear me?"

Carmine nodded, used to her mother's sermons—though this time her voice was sharper than usual, making Carmine wonder if she should fear something in particular. Had her mother heard of bandits? A child gone missing in another village? But she didn't dare question her irritable mother and kept nodding, being the good little girl she was expected to be.

She hadn't seen her grandmother for at least three months, so she was happy to go visit her, though her illness troubled her. Her grandmother had always been so strong, so healthy, thanks to her witchcraft. Even if she wasn't a healer, she knew how to brew potions that cured many ailments. She probably had something more serious than a cold for her to seek the help of Ozaryn's healer. What if she had caught the flu? Carmine's stomach clenched at the thought of her grandmother dying of the disease. Without hesitation, she put the remedy and the cake inside her basket, and left for her grandmother's house.

The walk from Ozaryn to Alverton, the village where her grandmother lived, took only an hour and even less time through the forest, unless a wild beast caught you and ensured your detour lasted an eternity. Carmine knew better than taking an ill-advised shortcut and like her mother had instructed her, stuck to the main road.

She was halfway to Alverton when a familiar voice called her name. At first she couldn't place it, but when the voice called her name a second time, she recognized it. It was the soothing voice she had heard in her dream.

Chapter Three

Now

"I'll go find the carcass myself then," Carmine said. "The crows can't have eaten it all already."

"Not today," her husband replied. "Laurel said you need to rest."

She opened her mouth to argue, but remained silent. Dacien was right. The healer, Laurel, had applied an ointment to her back to relieve the pain and speed up the healing process, but Carmine was still recovering. It would be foolish to go into the forest so soon. She knew her urge to retrieve the carcass and deal with the she-wolf wasn't reasonable. It was her pride talking, and she needed to silence it if she wanted to live another day.

Dacien offered to apply more of the ointment the healer had left behind.

"I'm not an expert in magical tattoos," he said as he gently massaged her back, "but I don't think your spell will keep working well with these injuries. The lines are broken in several places where the wolf clawed your skin."

If Carmine hadn't been lying on her stomach and cautious not to move her back muscles, she would have shrugged. "It didn't protect me from the she-wolf in the first place," she said.

"That's because it protected you from the other wolf before. The magic hadn't had time to… regenerate, if that's the right word for it. That's what your grandmother explained to me, but I can't recall her exact words."

"Maybe," Carmine said absentmindedly.

"Regardless, you should get it fixed," he said matter-of-factly, his face neutral. "I can't let you go on more hunts without it."

"And why not?" she asked. "I can handle myself. I repelled the she-wolf without the help of magic."

"You almost *died*, Carmine," Dacien said, exhaling. He was a patient man, but he wasn't used to Carmine disagreeing with him. She wasn't used to it either, but today was different. The tattoo was a topic Carmine discussed only with her grandmother, until her passing. Not with her husband, who wasn't versed in magic.

"But I didn't," she said with a hint of brashness in her voice. "And *you* don't have a magical tattoo to protect you from wolves."

"It isn't the same, and you know it."

She sighed. He didn't have to say the words for her to know what he meant. Carmine was a good huntress, but she was a woman. She was weaker. Less endurant. Her technique was excellent, but she needed the additional protection for "her own good," as he had repeated so many times. "My grandmother is dead anyway," she finally said. "I can't bring her back from the dead to fix the tattoo."

"She isn't the only witch in the region. You could ask your great-aunt."

"No. Not Aunt Ezélise." Not only did Carmine have no desire to travel to the other side of the region where her great-aunt lived, but her grandmother had always distrusted her younger sister. She used to tell Carmine that Aunt Ezélise practiced a bad kind of witchcraft that would corrupt Carmine's soul. And it wasn't only her grandmother who distrusted Aunt Ezélise. She had been chased from several villages and now lived in a cabin in the middle of the woods by herself, and the people from the nearby towns warned their children against the evil witch in the woods. "I don't want to see her."

"Then another one," Dacien said, throwing his hands in the air, an uncommon emotional display from him. Getting the tattoo fixed seemed very important to him, so important that Carmine wondered if there was another reason beyond her safety.

"There is no other one," Carmine snapped. A half-truth. There were probably other witches in the region, but none she knew, and none she could trust. Only her grandmother had known what had happened to her and why she had needed the spell in the first place, long before becoming a huntress. "We'll have to trust that the spell still works despite the damage to the tattoo, and if it doesn't, then I'll rely on my training. *Your* training."

"It won't be enough," Dacien said, before adding really quickly before Carmine could argue, "I won't insist for now. You need to rest. But I want you to think about it."

She exhaled and nodded slowly. Fine, she would think about it. And to be truthful, she had enjoyed the protection from the spell, especially how it had kept her scent hidden from wolves. But she would *not* give up hunting. Even if the spell didn't work anymore. It was her profession, her calling. Hunting, and hunting wolves in particular, was her way to reclaim her destiny and overcome her fears. Dacien, most of all, should understand that. It had been *his* idea. That's why she winced in surprise when he said, "Anyway, you should take a break. Not just to recover. A long break from hunting, so you can focus on more important things."

"What do you mean?" she asked, frowning. "What's more important than hunting? It's how we earn our livelihood."

"I can earn it for the two of us," he said firmly, but not unkindly. "I need you to focus on our family."

Carmine gritted her teeth, doing her best not to let her frustration show on her face. *Our family.* Despite his wishes, fatherhood eluded Dacien, and it was not for lack of trying. Carmine had not become pregnant yet, and though she had never told Dacien, it was a relief. Most women of her age had already surrendered to motherhood, and she didn't envy them. She even suspected that other women envied *her*, the huntress, who earned her own money and was free of the burden of caring for precious, vulnerable little humans. Of course, Carmine wondered why she wasn't with child yet, and had even wondered for a time if something was wrong with her body. Dacien had never insinuated it, and was good at pretending he wasn't upset each time she bled the lack of pregnancy out of her body, but Carmine still felt odd about it. Relieved, foremost, but also confused. Why did her body refuse to accomplish what it was supposed to?

She watched him silently, unable to formulate a response that wouldn't start an argument—the last thing she wanted. His face was neutral again, as it often was. Over the years since their marriage, she had learned to recognize the subtle signs that betrayed his emotions—a pinched lip for anger, slightly rounded eyes for happiness—but it still felt like trying to understand someone speaking another language.

Eventually, he leaned forward and said, kissing her forehead, "As soon as you feel better, we'll try again."

Carmine tensed. She had no desire to try again. But perhaps it was because of what had happened over the last twenty-four hours. Her mind was too busy recovering from her near-death experience to think about bringing a new life to Ozaryn. Or maybe she had already grown tired of Dacien's attempts to plant a seed inside her womb.

She still loved him—at least she thought so—but she was becoming distant, as if she couldn't allow herself to fully love Dacien anymore. It was no fault of his own, she knew. He had cared for her since the day they met, when she was still an adolescent and him a young man in his early twenties. He had always been patient, understanding, and loving after everything she went through. But like today, she had seen cracks in his patience recently, and feared it would only exacerbate her own reluctance to be the wife he had hoped she would become. She didn't say a thing about it, and simply smiled at Dacien before turning to her side and closing her eyes.

She spent the next three days lying in bed, her sleep interrupted by Dacien applying more ointment on her back, the daily visits of the healer, and Alandra bringing them food. Alandra had convinced her husband to pay half of the agreed price, trusting Carmine had killed the wolf and would bring proof of it. The money allowed Dacien to buy a new leather jacket for Carmine, which surprised her as she only used her old one for hunting, and he didn't want her to hunt anymore. Perhaps it was his way to soften the blow, or to promise the pause would only be temporary—just the time of a pregnancy and a few months caring for a newborn.

On the fourth day, the wounds had closed and her skin was healing up well. All she needed, she thought, was one more night of sleep, then her bed rest would finally be over. In the evening, Dacien joined her in bed for the first time since the attack, but didn't ask her to *try again*. She quickly fell asleep under his gaze, eager to wake up in the morning and resume the course of her life.

Carmine had hoped for a dreamless night, but her racing mind decided otherwise. Except this time, she didn't believe her mind was responsible for her eerie dream. She was familiar with common themes haunting her subconscious, but the last time she had dreamt of wolves and heard their song was ten years ago, and she had almost died because of it. And though the she-wolf hadn't spoken when trying to kill her a few days ago, the singing wolf in the new dream looked exactly the same.

Chapter Four

Then

The girl had long jet-black hair, olive skin, and lips red like blood. Her name was Carmine, the wolf knew, because he was a dream-walker and had visited her mind. She lived with her parents in Ozaryn, a village he sometimes visited when people couldn't recognize him for what he was. There, the day before, he had observed the girl. Never talked to her, of course, for her mother would have noticed. But today, she was walking near the woods he called home, and he could freely speak to her.

"Carmine," he called from behind.

She kept walking, as if she hadn't heard him. Was she ignoring him, the little brat? He called her again, and this time, she stopped and turned around. Finally, she listened! Her eyes stopped on him and his reddish fur. She froze, as if unable to decide if he was friend or foe. He moved closer, but she snapped out of her stupefaction and took a step back, putting her basket in front of her as if shielding herself from him.

He stopped moving and gently bowed, before saying, "I didn't mean to scare you, Carmine."

"How do you know my name?" she asked very fast, taking another step back. "And why do you speak?"

"Some wolves speak," he replied, realizing she didn't know what he—and thus, *she*—was. He hadn't expected it, but it wasn't an issue. He would soon show her. "And I know your name because I visited you in your dreams."

She frowned, then her face relaxed. *Good,* the wolf thought. *She remembers.* Sometimes the maidens forgot their dreams, and it made the approach more complicated.

"I knew your voice sounded familiar," she said.

"Did you like my song?"

She glanced around her and nodded carefully, as if she knew she was doing something wrong by talking to a stranger—but a stranger not for much longer, the wolf told himself, smiling inwardly. It made the whole situation even more delightful.

He slowly approached her and asked, "Would you like to hear it again?"

"I don't know," she said with a shaky voice, squeezing the basket against her.

The girl was becoming wary again. His approach was too direct. "Another time, then," he said. "I could visit your dream again next month."

She didn't answer immediately, thinking, but eventually said, "Why not sooner?"

"Because she won't be ready until next month," he said, looking up at the sky.

"She?"

"The moon. I can only visit maidens' dreams when she's full."

Carmine blushed. Was it the word "maiden" that had caused her reaction? She was young, the wolf knew. Becoming a woman with every passing day since she had bled, but still an adolescent. So young, so innocent, and so *ready*. He would ensure she transformed into the being she was supposed to become, no matter what it would take. No matter if she agreed to it or not. Because in the end, once she tasted her new existence, she wouldn't regret it. None of the maidens ever did. Even he himself had refused his fate at first, back when he was a young stripling, only to better embrace it when another dream-walker had made him see reason.

"Then I'll see you next month," she said, bowing her head politely. Then, hesitantly, she straightened up and moved her basket to her side. "Now, if you excuse me, I need to keep going."

He could have let her go and tried again later, but in truth, he didn't want to wait one more month. "Do you still have a long journey?" he asked pressingly. "I would be happy to accompany you a little, if you desire so."

She gulped uneasily. "Thank you, but that won't be necessary. I'm almost there."

"Are you going to Alverton?" he asked. Carmine didn't respond. Which could only mean that he had aptly guessed her destination. "Do you have family in town?"

"My grandmother," she said. "She's a very influential and powerful woman. She's expecting me any time now."

Carmine had spoken with a firm tone, emphasizing the words *influential* and *powerful*. The wolf had heard it before. Women often lied about who they visited or lived with, in the vain hope that men would leave them alone, too scared to anger a jealous husband or a protective father—or an influential old woman who was supposedly powerful enough to scare him.

"She's a witch," she added.

Probably another lie, the wolf told himself. Witches and druids couldn't find suitable apprentices anymore, and they were slowly but surely disappearing from the world. Soon only the purest form of magic would survive without humans to interfere with it.

"Where does she reside? I have been looking for a witch for a long time," he lied. "I would love to visit her sometime soon. Perhaps you could tell her about me, so she doesn't chase me away when I come to ask her for a potion."

She bit her lip and looked down, visibly embarrassed. He had been right, the wolf thought. The girl's grandmother was no witch and was probably not influential or powerful either.

"She is... not able to receive customers at this time," Carmine said at last. "She has a cold."

Exactly what he thought. Just an old, sick woman waiting for her granddaughter to visit her in her old, dusty house. "I can visit her in a few days, when she feels better."

"I don't know..." she said. Then she clenched her fists and added, "I really need to go now."

"Please, just tell me where I can find your grandmother. I promise I won't bother her anytime soon, and I won't bother you any longer after you tell me."

Carmine sighed, and finally said, "She lives in the red house on the town's western border."

"Thank you," the wolf said. "I wish you safe travels, Carmine. I will sing for you again next month."

With that, he disappeared into the woods and ran as quickly as he could toward Alverton, hoping to dispose of the old woman before the girl's arrival. A pillow pressed against her face would end her life quickly. Finding her grandmother dead, Carmine would have no choice but to walk back home to tell her parents, and this time, the wolf would make himself more convincing to lure her away from the path, using her distress to his advantage.

He was breathless when he arrived at the red-bricked house. On the door was a sign that read "Ezilda's shop." It was quiet, and there was no smoke coming from the chimney. Could the old woman have gone to the village healer to get help with her cold? Scratching on the door with his right paw, the wolf asked if there was anyone inside. When nobody answered him, he opened the door. Inside, he found shelves of books, vials, and dried herbs. An empty cauldron sat on the dusty wooden floor next to a broom. Perhaps the woman was a witch after all. Or just an herbalist, and her granddaughter had elevated her to the rank of witchcraft practitioner, only to scare him away. But he wasn't scared. He was excited.

Of all the scenarios the wolf had run in his mind before meeting Carmine, he had never imagined the one that was unfolding naturally before his eyes. A bed. A thick blanket. An absent grandmother leaving room for a false one. Yes, this was obvious. He didn't have to lure the girl back into the woods to achieve his goal. She would come to him willingly, and once faced with the true nature of the individual in the bedsheets, she would have no choice but to surrender to him. The old woman would have made a tasty snack, but her absence made everything easier.

Inside the wardrobe, he found a checkered dress and a white nightcap that he quickly put on. Then, a wicked smile on his face, he slipped into the bed. It felt warm under the blanket, and he couldn't wait for the girl to join him. He was about to have the most delicious time of his life, so delicious that he was already drooling in anticipation.

Hiding his furry body under the blanket, he waited. It was only a matter of time before Carmine knocked on the door and joined him in bed for her awakening.

Chapter Five

Now

Carmine lay in bed awake, staring at the ceiling and listening to Dacien's slow respiration. The fire he had lit up in the hearth last night had already gone out, but Carmine still felt hot. Her body and mind were burning.

Another dream-walker had visited her sleep. One that had tried to kill her *before* invading her dreams. Carmine had pointlessly tried, in the dream, to cover her ears not to hear the song. *You are my sister*, the dream-walker sang, *and the blue moon is your mother*. These words, again. Meaningless. Soothing then, terrifying now. Only when the dream-walker had approached her, getting close, so close, Carmine had finally managed to jolt herself awake, her heart about to explode in her chest. Why hadn't it—or rather, *she*—spoken during their fight in the forest? *Unless,* Carmine thought, *it was just a dream.* Perhaps her mind was playing tricks on her.

Doubt still pervaded her thoughts, so she left the bed, careful not to wake Dacien, and looked through the window. The moon was full. *A coincidence,* she told herself. Dream-walkers were a myth, her grandmother had told her. The wolf who had almost killed her ten years ago was only a stray beast enchanted beyond reason by an irresponsible druid, and it had never visited her sleep. The dream had been a mere coincidence. Her memory of the wolf mentioning the dream was only a result of her traumatized mind trying to make sense of her ordeal. But now that she had dreamt of wolves a second time in such an eerily similar way, she doubted that explanation again. What if she had remembered correctly? What if dream-walkers were real?

Now Carmine had two reasons to go back into the forest. She had to find the carcass of the sheep-killer—or whatever was left of it—then find the she-wolf and confront it. And she would be prepared this time. Nothing Dacien could say would stop her. Protective spell working or not, she needed answers, and she would get them. Quietly, she put her new leather jacket and the rest of her hunting attire on and left the safety of her house for the bitter cold of the early fall morning.

The sun was barely peeking over the horizon, but the full moon added a bit of brightness to the skies, just enough to guide Carmine. She knew where she was going. The she-wolf could be anywhere, but the carcass should still be near the den. Not right where she had killed the wolf, since the men who had tried to retrieve the carcass had been unsuccessful, but it couldn't be far. And perhaps she could track the she-wolf from there, too.

Before anyone in Ozaryn could see her, Carmine disappeared among the trees. Songbirds covered the sound of the dead orangey leaves crunching under her footsteps, heavier than usual. Her back still ached, altering her normally light and agile gait. Carefully listening over the chirping, she hurried through the forest until she reached the den. It was only when she saw that the wolf's carcass was gone, as the men had told her, that she realized her heart pounded in her chest with a fury she hadn't felt in a decade. Even when the she-wolf had attacked her in this very place a few days ago, she hadn't reacted so intensely. The last time her heart had tried to leap out of her chest, she was fourteen and a wolf was trying to devour her.

But Carmine was alone now, and not defenseless like she had been ten years ago. Why did she feel so heavy, as if she was about to collapse under her own weight? She brought a hand to her chest and exhaled as slowly as she could, trying to slow down her racing heart. It didn't make sense. She was fine. The big bad wolf was dead. And the she-wolf wasn't a dream-walker. There was no such thing as dream-walkers. She would find the she-wolf and plant an arrow inside its heart and be done with it.

Taking a deep breath in, she crouched and went inside the den. The carcass wasn't there, but what she found was intriguing all the same. Roughly cut pieces of leather and wool clothing were spread across the ground, as if the den's inhabitant had made itself a soft bed. A shiver went down Carmine's spine. Had the wolf killed people and brought their clothes to its den after devouring their flesh? No, she would have heard about it if people had gone missing after wandering into the woods. The wolf must have found the clothes abandoned somewhere. And regardless of what it had done, it was gone. She had seen death overcome the beast after her own knife sunk into its neck.

Carmine left the den and pursued her exploration of the area, still hoping to find the carcass, or at least some bones to prove the animal's death. She carefully examined the den's surroundings until she found her first clue. Something had disturbed the ground close to where she had killed the wolf, and she could even see traces in the dirt indicating that the corpse had been dragged away. Perhaps a hungry bear had found and brought it to its den to feast one last time before hibernating. She wasn't keen on disrupting a bear's sleep to retrieve the wolf's remains, but she still followed the trail.

The sun rose high in the sky when Carmine reached the end of the muddy trail, warming her skin pleasantly. It led to a clearing she and Dacien often used to seek reprieve from long, exhausting hunts. Sunbeams flooded the middle of the clearing, where Dacien had placed loose tree trunks for him and Carmine to sit on. She couldn't find enough evidence of stomped grass or other disturbances that she usually looked for when tracking animals. A dead end. Not ready to give up yet, she kept searching until her eyes stopped on something unusual. On the other side of the clearing, beyond the trunks, something white was carefully placed on an unnatural mound. Approaching it, she realized the white item was a bouquet of lilies, and the mound on which it rested, a grave. Nothing else besides the flowers marked it. Who was this unfortunate man or woman buried anonymously in the middle of nowhere? A thought crossed her mind. What if it wasn't someone, but... the wolf she had killed? Perhaps it had really fled from a druid's captivity, and its former master had found and buried its remains here, in the forest.

She had to confirm her suspicion. She kneeled on the ground and started digging the grave with her bare hands. After breaking a nail in her haste and covering the others in dirt, she finally found something. Something that didn't have fur at all. She uncovered a leg. An unmistakable *human* leg and the dozens of worms that covered its greenish skin. Resisting the urge to vomit, she quickly buried it again, silently cursing herself for trespassing in the last resting place of that poor soul. What if she had disturbed the deceased's rest, who would then curse her? This was probably mere superstition, but Carmine couldn't help but recall the stories her mother told her of grave robbers cursed by the dead.

She was halfway done packing dirt back onto the grave, whispering apologies to the deceased, when she heard a sound that made her freeze.

A growl.

Slowly, she grabbed her bow and turned her head toward the sound.

A lean brown creature was approaching, its yellowish eyes fixing Carmine like a predator focused on its prey. The she-wolf was back, and it looked furious.

Carmine readied herself to shoot, but before she could attach the arrow to the bowstring, the she-wolf stopped growling. Then she sat and said, her voice low and bitter, "How dare you touch him?"

Heavens, this is real, Carmine told herself. The she-wolf spoke with a human-like voice. She must have visited her dream... Quickly, Carmine rose and took a step back before saying, "I buried him again when I realized my mistake."

"And what a huge mistake it was," the she-wolf said, rising and approaching the grave languidly. "One I don't understand how someone like you could make."

Carmine kept walking backward, her bow still drawn and ready to shoot at the first sign of aggression from the she-wolf. The dream-walker would already be dead if it—if *she*, since this wasn't a mere wolf—if she hadn't spoken, and if Carmine wasn't burning with curiosity only a conversation with this dangerous creature could extinguish.

At last, the dream-walker placed herself between the grave and Carmine. "Go away and never come back. Let him rest in peace under her light."

"Her light?"

The dream-walker lifted her head and said, staring at the sky, "Her pale majesty the moon. His mother, and mine. And *yours*, you stupid girl."

"What are you talking about?" Carmine asked.

"So it's true," the dream-walker said. "You don't know."

Anger rose inside Carmine's chest. What sick game was this evil creature playing? "I don't know what you mean, but I won't trust the words of a beast who almost killed me and invaded my dreams."

The dream-walker tilted her head. "So at least you remember the dreams."

"Every bit of it," Carmine spat. "And how your kind uses them to trick innocent little girls into deadly traps."

"You don't look like a little girl to me."

Carmine snorted. "Another one like you tried to eat me ten years ago. He hid inside my grandmother's house. Even slipped inside her bed to cover himself. Then he tried devouring me."

"So it was you," the dream-walker said, her cold, amber eyes lighting up as she visibly understood something. "You were the maiden this idiot tried to take by force."

"Don't call me that," Carmine said, feeling sick as she remembered the big bad wolf pronouncing the word "maiden" to her face as if she were a piece of meat.

"You may not be a maiden anymore by human standards, but you're still one to us," the dream-walker said.

"I don't care about your beastly standard," Carmine said. "I don't associate with child-eaters."

The dream-walker let out a soft, sarcastic laugh. "My dear, he wasn't trying to eat you."

"And how would you know? I was there. I know what happened."

"If you know so well, perhaps you should ask that husband of yours what happened that day, and why you were stalked and supposedly almost eaten by a wolf."

"Dacien saved me!" Carmine shouted. Her hands trembled, struggling to keep the bow raised toward the dream-walker.

"Oh, he did for sure," the dream-walker said. "My cousin deserved the price he paid. One should *not* awaken a maiden without her consent. He was about to take away your freedom to choose. But your husband ended up doing exactly the same. He hid the truth from you and turned you against us. He even used magic, I believe. I couldn't smell you nor walk your dreams until today. Am I right, maiden?"

Magic? No, Dacien was no magician. It was her grandmother's spell the dream-walker was talking about. "My grandmother, not Dacien, put a protective spell on my back," she reluctantly admitted. "To protect me from wolves, after *your cousin* tried to kill me."

"And to protect you from becoming yourself."

Carmine remained silent. The dream-walker's words were like a poison slowly infiltrating her mind and impregnating it with doubt. She should have been strong and ended the unnatural creature's life as soon as it had opened its deceptive fang-filled mouth. But Carmine couldn't stop listening. The carefully chosen words coming out of the dream-walker's mouth sounded sincere and told Carmine it would be ill-advised to ignore them, no matter if she believed them or not.

"Haven't you wondered why he doesn't have the same protective spell? He's a hunter, isn't he? We are a threat to him, too."

Of course I have, Carmine thought. "Magic isn't free," she said very fast. "It costs a lot of resources. It draws a lot of energy from a witch to cast a spell, and magical ink isn't commonly available. I needed the spell, and my husband didn't. He is"—it pained her to say it, but it was true—"a better hunter than I am."

"Nonsense," the dream-walker said firmly, her voice raising. "You're the strongest hunter I have ever encountered. I inflicted severe injuries on your body, and you kept fighting me. No one has offered me such resistance before."

Carmine fell silent again. She had been strong indeed during their first encounter. She had survived when most would have perished. It was difficult to admit it, but the dream-walkers' words rang true. She had questions for Dacien. As she stared at the dream-walker, thinking, the creature looked at the grave and scratched the ground to finish reburying the dead man.

"Who was he?" Carmine eventually asked.

"Another idiot," the dream-walker said bitterly, "except this one didn't deserve to die for his foolishness."

Chapter Six

Then

Carmine found the door of her grandmother's house closed. Not ajar; well and truly closed. Carmine bit her lower lip. The witch always kept it open during the day to welcome customers inside her shop. But she was sick, Carmine knew, and must have closed her business for the day. That was surely it. No need to panic over a closed door, right?

She knocked on the door while saying, "Grandmother, it's me, Carmine."

"You can come in," a strange voice said from inside. For a second, Carmine wondered who it belonged to. A visitor, perhaps? Then she realized that her grandmother's voice was probably hoarse because of her disease. "The door is unlocked."

Carmine entered the house. Her grandmother was in bed under a pile of blankets as if she was trying to warm herself, but strangely, no fire burned in the hearth. Perhaps she was too weak to light one up. But too weak to even use witchcraft to start the fire? This was odd, but perhaps she was really, really sick.

"Mother told me you were unwell," Carmine said, "so I brought a cake, and a remedy made by Ozaryn's healer."

"This is kind of you," her grandmother's muffled voice came from under the blankets. "Please put everything on the table."

Carmine did as she was told, ignoring the inner voice telling her how odd her grandmother's voice sounded, even if it was caused by a sore throat.

"Would you be kind and light up a fire?" her grandmother asked. "I'm very cold."

"Of course," Carmine said, putting logs into the hearth. She found an ember from the previous night and added tinder on it to reignite the flame.

"Now please join me in bed to help me warm up."

What an odd request! Carmine's heart sped up, her intuition once again sparking with uncertainty. But her grandmother had always been different from others, hadn't she? She was a witch. Not a mere old lady spoiling her grandchildren with candy. She loved Carmine differently, telling her stories of magic and potions and enchanted forests. And, of course, always hugging her with the tenderest of affections once story time was over. Surely she would feel better with her granddaughter next to her, and Carmine had no reason to refuse.

Carmine climbed onto the bed. Her grandmother laid on her side, her back facing Carmine. She wore her nightclothes and a nightcap that covered her hair. Huddled as she was, she looked small and frail, as if she was trying to disappear under the blankets.

"What is the sickness afflicting you, grandmother?" Carmine asked, worried.

Her grandmother didn't answer. Carmine wondered if she had fallen asleep, so she moved her hand to touch her shoulder, but before she reached her, her grandmother turned, revealing a face devoid of humanity. The face of a wolf. And not any wolf. The talking wolf she had just met on the road to Alverton.

"You took your time," he said with a deep, husky voice that sounded this way not because of illness, but because he looked eerily excited.

Carmine couldn't move. She stared at the wolf's long, sharp teeth that filled his giant mouth—a mouth twisted into a smile that she didn't know wolves could have. Even as he licked his chops excitedly, she found herself unable to scream or push him away.

As she was staring at him and feeling her heart explode inside her chest, he approached her ear and whispered, "You look delicious, maiden."

A single tear rolled down her cheek. He was about to devour her, and her body was betraying her, unable to move to save her life. But even if she tried running away, where would she go? Wolves ran faster than young girls, and she didn't know where her grandmother was—if she was still alive and not in the beast's belly already.

It was over. She would never hug her grandmother—the real one—again. Her friends in Ozaryn would ask her parents what happened to her, and once told a wolf had eaten her, they would cry for a day or two before moving on with their lives, making new friends that would replace her. Her parents would maybe miss her, but probably not, and would only be reminded of her past existence when customers would ask about the shoemaker's daughter.

"Don't worry, I'll change into something you like better," the wolf said.

She barely had time to think about what he said when she heard muffled voices outside of the house. Someone was coming. It gave her the strength she needed, and she finally let out the scream that had been trapped inside her throat.

The door burst open, letting her grandmother and a young man carrying a bow and an axe inside the house.

"No!" Carmine's grandmother shouted as she saw the wolf dangerously lean over Carmine with his jaw wide open. "You will *not* touch her, you beast!"

The young man who had entered behind the witch reacted in a heartbeat and threw himself at the wolf, his axe ready to smash the wolf's head. Carmine was still screaming when the wolf jumped at the man before he could reach the bed, and they fell to the floor in a deadly embrace. The wolf growled and snapped and scratched as the man held him against the floor, the axe's handle pressed hard against his throat. The man was struggling against a fury of teeth and claws and muscle, but he didn't let go.

After a few seconds that felt like hours to Carmine, her grandmother whispered an incantation that paralyzed the wolf long enough for the man to slit the animal's throat with his axe. The wolf convulsed on the floor before his eyes stopped moving and went blank as the permanence of death seized him.

An eerie silence filled the room. The man—a hunter, Carmine realized—was hurt. He had bleeding scratches all over his face and his clothing was slashed in multiple places. But he didn't complain. He quietly lifted the wolf's dead body and carried it outside of the house. As he walked out, blood dripped from the wolf's throat, painting the wooden floor in a crimson trail. Carmine knew she shouldn't watch, but she couldn't help herself. The absolute terror that had paralyzed her before her grandmother and the hunter saved her was slowly being replaced by relief and admiration. This man hadn't hesitated one second before risking his life to defend her from a gigantic beast almost as heavy as himself. Without him, she would be dead.

Carmine's grandmother sat next to her on the bed. Her eyes were dull and sad. She didn't look sick, Carmine noticed, but she did look exhausted. It must have been the magic she used to help the hunter kill the wolf.

"Please tell me we arrived before he could hurt you," her grandmother whispered.

Carmine looked down. Her body was intact. No bite, scratch, or other injury like the hunter had suffered while fighting the wolf. They had arrived before he could snap her neck and tear her flesh apart. She nodded.

"Why did your mother send you alone? What did she think would happen?"

Carmine didn't know how to respond to her grandmother's accusatory tone. She had traveled alone between Ozaryn and Alverton several times, and had never run into trouble. Why did her grandmother suddenly blame her mother for being irresponsible, when she had never raised an eyebrow about it in the past?

But Carmine didn't have to reply, because her grandmother embraced her and said, "I'm so sorry I wasn't home when you arrived, Carmine. I will never let another wolf try taking you away from me. I won't let it happen."

An uncontrollable wave of tears finally flooded Carmine's face. She didn't speak and sobbed silently against her grandmother's chest for a long, sorrowful moment. After a while, the hunter came back inside the house. He carried a shovel and his arms were covered in dirt. *He must have buried the wolf,* Carmine told herself as she glanced at him with watery eyes. His stature and demeanor impressed her. His face was relaxed and his voice calm when he asked Carmine's grandmother what else she needed. He acted as if he wasn't bothered by his injuries or by the blood dripping from his clothes, and was ready to fight a dozen more beasts. Carmine wondered if all hunters were like him.

Her grandmother helped her lie down and said softly, "Get some rest, my child. I need to tend to Dacien's injuries. Then I will make us rabbit stew with mushrooms."

"Aren't you sick?" Carmine asked. "Mother said to bring—"

"I have recovered already," her grandmother said with a meek smile. "Now, stop worrying about me and get some rest."

Carmine wanted to ask more questions about her illness, but her grandmother was right. She looked perfectly fine, as if whatever ailment had plagued her was long gone. Perhaps the news of her disease had reached Ozaryn too late, or her mother had worried for nothing. But it didn't matter. Her grandmother was healthy and not about to die. Nothing else mattered to Carmine, now that she was safe.

So she relented and lay down, quietly watching her grandmother heal the hunter's injuries with her magic. She whispered incantations and applied ointments on his wounds, while the hunter silently watched her work, briefly glancing at Carmine occasionally. He was older than her, but still a young man. She had never seen him in Ozaryn. Later, as they ate the rabbit stew, she learned he was from Alverton and had left the village five years ago, on his sixteenth birthday. He had gone to pursue training in the city, learning from a master hunter who had kindly agreed to take him under his wing. Now he was back in town and helped the villagers with their needs, from game meat to wolf pelts. He even protected the village's only witch by escorting her deep into the forest as she gathered rare ingredients for potions. Carmine's grandmother hadn't expected to see her granddaughter so early, she explained. She apologized one more time for not being home when Carmine arrived, letting a wicked wolf take her place inside the bed. At least she had the ingredients she wanted, and she would even use some of them for a spell for Carmine.

"What spell?" Carmine said softly.

"A magical tattoo," her grandmother said. "My most powerful magic. It will protect you from these evil beasts."

"From talking wolves?"

"Yes, from *all* wolves, talking or not," she said. She explained to Carmine how wolves would be unable to smell or track her, and how the tattoo would protect her in case she still encountered one. "As long as my magic is with you, they won't be able to harm you."

Carmine spent the rest of the day resting in bed while her grandmother and the hunter went outside the house. She could still hear their muffled voices, assuring her they were right behind the door and hadn't left her alone at the mercy of other ravenous beasts. They sounded absorbed in a long conversation that she couldn't understand, for they spoke with low, careful voices. She only caught snippets about wolves and magic. The hunter spoke little, as if he was only asking questions, but already she felt reassured by the sound of his voice. She later asked them what they had discussed. The hunter remained silent, glancing apprehensively at Carmine's grandmother. The witch seemed hesitant at first, but after Carmine pressed her one more time, she said the hunter had convinced her to let him teach Carmine the skills she would need to fend off the wild animals living in the forest. On these promising words, Carmine closed her eyes and enjoyed a heavy, dreamless sleep.

The next day, the hunter helped Carmine's grandmother prepare the enchanted ink she would need to make the tattoo. Then, as Carmine lay on her stomach while her grandmother readied the needle, she grabbed his hand and braced herself for the incoming pain, vowing to never let herself become the prey of any beast.

Chapter Seven

Now

So dream-walkers were real, after all.

The she-wolf's mysterious, eerie words haunted Carmine as she walked back to the village. *Maiden. Moon. Mother.* The dream-walker had told Carmine how the two most important people in her life—her grandmother and her husband—had lied to her, yet she had refused to elaborate, sending her to question Dacien instead. She had refused to tell her who the buried man was, or what the other dream-walker—the big bad wolf—had truly wanted, if not to eat her. What a wicked, tormenting beast she was! She seemed to revel in planting seeds of doubt and confusion inside Carmine's mind. But what Carmine dreaded even more was the possibility of the dream-walker being not only cryptic, but truthful. It would have been so much easier to dismiss everything she had said and kill her, but something told Carmine she would have been deeply wrong to do so.

Carmine crossed from the forest into Ozaryn, the town already awake and bustling. She found Dacien in front of their house speaking with Alandra and other villagers, a concerned look on his face. It quickly faded as he saw her, and she realized he must have been looking for her after finding her side of the bed cold and empty.

"Where were you?" he asked, his voice higher than usual and his brows slightly furrowed, betraying a blend of relief and annoyance. The others left, their presence not needed anymore.

"Just taking a stroll on the edge of the forest." He opened his mouth to protest, but she added very quickly, "I feel fine, Dacien. And I didn't go very far."

"With your hunting attire on," he said, sounding suspicious.

She nodded. "I didn't go far, but I still didn't want to take any chances. I'd rather be ready and not need it than the opposite."

Her answer seemed to satisfy him enough because he nodded before walking inside the house, and she followed him. Without a word, he set up the table for breakfast with bread, cheese, and dried fruits from the pantry, while she took off her leather jacket and hunting gear, thinking about what to ask him, and how.

"You remember that wolf who tried eating me all those years ago?" she said as they ate.

"Of course I do," he answered. "What about it?"

"Why didn't it attack me when it first encountered me on the road to Alverton?"

Dacien frowned before answering, "Perhaps it worried another traveler would hear you scream, come to your rescue, and kill it."

Carmine snorted softly. Ironically, it was exactly what had happened in the end—Dacien had heard her scream inside her grandmother's house and rescued her, killing the wolf in the process. But it was sheer luck that he had come back in time. If he had still been away, deep in the forest alongside Carmine's grandmother gathering her ingredients, Carmine could have screamed all she wanted and nobody would have heard her. Not even her grandmother's neighbors, for they didn't live close enough to the red-bricked house. Witches liked their privacy, and Carmine's grandmother had been no exception.

"Possibly," she conceded.

"Why do you ask?"

Carmine gulped. "I've been thinking about what happened again, after the she-wolf attacked me. It... brought back memories."

"The wolf is dead. It can't come back to hurt you," Dacien said, not unkindly.

"I know," she said, sighing, "but these two attacks were so... different. The she-wolf didn't hesitate to jump at me the second it saw me. While that other talking wolf—"

"An unnatural, evilly enchanted beast."

"Yes." She repressed the urge to tell him about dream-walkers, and that the she-wolf was one, too. She didn't know if he lied to her or not, but if he did, she preferred to feign ignorance. "That other wolf convinced me to share where I was going, and once it was inside my grandmother's house, it lured me into the bed before revealing its true nature, when it could have simply attacked after I closed the door."

Dacien stared at her, silent. At last, he sighed and said, "Do you expect me to explain that creature's wicked behavior?"

"I don't know," she said, shrugging. "Don't you find that odd, too?"

"Everything was odd about this wolf," he snapped, his pinched lip telling Carmine he was becoming upset. "I got rid of it. What's the point of ruminating on what happened?"

His patience was gone already, and the conversation had just started. Dacien had never shied away from discussing that fateful day in the past, but Carmine had never questioned the wolf's motive until now. She hated it, but Carmine started to believe the dream-walker. Something was wrong.

"What about the spell, Dacien? Why me, and not you?"

"We already discussed it," he said. "I don't need—"

"Why no one else? I have *never* heard of any other villager getting stalked by a talking wolf. Nobody else needs magical protection against wolves or any other beast."

Dacien clenched his fists. "Your grandmother believed the spell would help you recover faster from what had happened. That it would give you the confidence you needed to keep going on without fear of being attacked again. And that it would help you as a huntress, should you become one."

It sounded so logical, but also so wrong. His speech was fast and flat, almost automatic. As if he had learned what to say. Had he conspired with her grandmother? But for what?

"I dreamt of wolves again," she said, staring at him defiantly.

Dacien blinked. "What are you talking about?"

"Before the wolf attacked me ten years ago, I dreamt of it. Then, after my grandmother put the spell on me, I never dreamt of wolves again. Oh, I had a few nightmares about what had happened, but I never experienced a dream like the one I had before I met that wolf. Then, after the she-wolf hurt my back a few days ago, I dreamt of wolves again. I dreamt of the she-wolf, Dacien. Is that why you want me to get the tattoo fixed? So I can't dream of wolves?"

Dacien stared at her for a moment, visibly thinking about what to say.

Don't be a liar, she thought, wishing with all her heart for the dream-walker to be wrong.

But all the hope she had nurtured since talking to the dream-walker about Dacien being truthful died when he said, "I promised your grandmother not to say a word about it. For your own good."

A piece of Carmine's soul broke inside her. He had known something for all these years and never told her. Her own husband. Her savior.

"My own good," she said at last, her face puckering uncontrollably.

"I swear," he said. "Trust me, like you would trust your grandmother. She was the one who didn't want you to know the full extent of the spell."

Carmine raised her hand to make him stop talking. She was disgusted. It was so easy to blame the dead for his own lies. Her grandmother couldn't defend herself, share her version of the story, the truth about what she and Dacien had agreed on.

"Why do I dream of wolves?" she asked. "Why do I need to be protected against the dreams?"

He slowly shook his head. "It's... complicated, Carmine. I swore not to say a word."

"Do you have a magic spell preventing you from telling me?" she asked, raising an eyebrow sarcastically.

"No," he whispered.

"Then tell me," she said, putting her hand on his arm in an attempt to get closer to him emotionally—like they had been, many years ago, after marrying each other. "I need to know what danger hovers above me. Why did my grandmother pretend my dream wasn't special, yet she engraved her magic into my skin to protect me from more dreams of talking wolves?" Dacien looked at her with regretful eyes, so she pressed harder on his arm and added, her voice soft and low, "Why are dream-walkers trying to invade my mind at night during the full moon?"

Dacien put his own hand on hers. "I wish I could tell you," he said, sounding sincerely sorry. "But I must not."

"Why?" she said with imploring eyes. "Don't I deserve to know the truth?"

"Because it's too dangerous. If you knew... you could be tempted to try and then you couldn't go back, and you would regret it every single second of your life. That's why I need you to get the tattoo fixed. It's too tempting. Your grandmother knew it and wanted to protect you."

"To protect me against *myself*?" she said, remembering the dream-walker's words.

He nodded. "The human heart is weak and easily tempted by corruption when lured by power," he said. "A woman's heart, even more."

She quickly removed her hand, as if his touch had suddenly become scorching hot. *He was about to take away your freedom to choose,* the dream-walker had said to her about the big bad wolf. *But your husband ended up doing exactly the same.* But her freedom to choose what? To let wolves wander into her dreams? Whatever it was, Dacien had lied, and now that she was catching on, he still refused to tell her. Because he thought she was weak. What pained her even more was the thought of her beloved grandmother holding the same belief. Perhaps it was justified when she was fourteen, but not anymore. She didn't deserve to live the rest of her life in the dark.

"Tell me," she said, her voice loud and firm, but tears coming to her eyes. "My heart is *not* weak. I'm not a child anymore."

"No," he answered.

It was final. He wouldn't tell her. Her own husband still treated her like the child she was when he had met her. Dacien, the hunter who had let his wife learn his skills, who was kind and loving, was just another individual refusing to give her full control of her own destiny. Stifling the nausea coming up her throat, Carmine rose, grabbed her hunting knives, and left the house.

Chapter Eight

The beginning

The full moon shone proudly in the sky when Carmine's mother went into labor. It had already raised three times this season, making this fourth occurrence a rarity only astronomers cared about, and certainly not Carmine's mother as she painfully pushed her daughter into the world.

But astronomers were not the only ones staring at the moon tonight. Adepts of the dying magic arts were, too. One witch in particular looked through the window worryingly as she held her daughter's hand to help her endure the hardships of childbirth, while the healer held the emerging head of the infant they would soon name Carmine. The witch's name was Ezilda, and she dreaded telling her daughter that she had just birthed a cursed child. All hope wasn't lost, though. The baby girl was moon-marked, but the primal magic that lay inside her could be reined in by witchcraft. And they had time, for Carmine's powers would be dormant until another awoke them. Until then, she would remain human, and only human.

So Carmine came into the world moon-marked, dark-haired, and rosy-cheeked. Nobody could see the mark of the heavenly body on her skin, for it had marked upon her soul. Only witches and druids could sense it, and when the time would come, others like her. The supernatural scent was strong, intoxicating. It filled the air with an indescribable sourness Ezilda had never smelled before. Like having rusted metal in her mouth. She felt overwhelmed by it as her daughter took the newborn into her arms for the first time. She would have to tell her, but for now she let mother and daughter recover from the life-changing event that had just happened to both of them.

Later in the night, when the sun was just behind the horizon ready to outshine the moon, Ezilda summoned the newborn's father inside the healer's house. She let him meet his daughter, but soon she spoke about Carmine's fate.

"Dream-walkers aren't real," he said after Ezilda explained what being moon-marked meant. "My daughter isn't going to turn into a beast just because she was born tonight."

"If my mother says they are real, then they are," Carmine's mother replied, watching the infant sleeping on her breast with a blend of love and fear. "You must listen to her."

Carmine's father pouted. He had never trusted his mother-in-law, and acknowledged the existence of witchcraft only because the old woman had demonstrated her magical skills in convincing-enough ways. But that didn't mean every story she told about the full moon and monsters was real.

"How can others like her awaken her powers?" Carmine's mother asked.

Ezilda gently put her hand on her daughter's shoulder and said, "After she bleeds for the first time, others will start visiting her dreams on the full moon. They will poison her mind and make her believe they mean no harm to her, so they can slowly seduce her. One will set his sight on her, and will awaken her powers in the same way he will awaken her womanhood."

"What does that mean?" Carmine's father asked.

Ezilda gave him a grim smile. "When your daughter lies with another dream-walker, she will become one of them."

It was too much for Carmine's father to hear, so he left. Ezilda wasn't done, but she didn't hold him back. There was still plenty of time to protect Carmine from her fate.

"Tell me how to prevent my daughter from becoming one of these monsters," Carmine's mother pleaded. "There must be something you can do to stop this."

"There is indeed," Ezilda said.

"Let's do it now, then."

Ezilda shook her head. "We have to wait. My spell is too dangerous to cast on an infant, and it will not seal her powers if I cast it before she has her first menses. When she bleeds for the first time, send her to me immediately. I will put a magical tattoo on her that will protect her mind from dream-walking, and should she still lie with a dream-walker, her powers will not awaken."

Carmine's mother nodded, a veil of relief falling onto her face. She gently lifted Carmine toward her mother. Ezilda placed the infant against her chest and silently swore to the moon that she would never let her take her beloved granddaughter.

Chapter Nine

Now

Carmine felt defenseless going into the forest with leather shoes, linen clothes, and her hunting knives as sole companions, but she didn't care. She had stormed out of the house without a thought for her bow or warmer clothes, and now she was running toward the clearing, ignoring all the teachings she had ever received about wandering safely into the woods. Though the sun was high on the horizon already, the humidity of the forest pervaded Carmine's nose and throat without mercy, exacerbating the surrounding coldness her light clothes struggled to protect her from.

Please, still be there, she found herself wishing. The dream-walker had been right. The tattoo on her back wasn't a mere protection spell—or rather, it protected her against more than her grandmother had pretended. Carmine needed to know why Ezilda had prevented dream-walkers from visiting her dreams. Why she lied about their existence. Carmine needed answers, and if her husband wouldn't give them, then she would get them from someone else. Perhaps the she-wolf wouldn't be as cryptic this time.

The clearing was bathed in sunlight. Next to the unmarked grave wasn't the dream-walker, but a naked woman arranging the white flowers that covered it. Her long wavy hair was as black as a starless night and fell onto her body like an unearthly veil of shadow.

"I knew you would come back," she said, turning her head toward Carmine.

Carmine froze. Not only because the woman had mesmerizing eyes as black as her hair, but because she had the same voice as the she-wolf, and a scar on her right arm. "You are the dream-walker," she said softly, almost whispering. "The she-wolf."

"You're finally getting it," the woman said, a discreet smile on the corner of her lips.

Carmine felt blood flush her cheeks as her eyes went down from the woman's face to her naked body. *She is beautiful,* she thought, before chasing the lustful ideas away. She looked up again and asked, "Who are you?"

"You can call me Louve."

"Is that your real name?"

"Does it matter?" the woman said, cocking her head. "Don't you have better questions than what my parents may or may not have called me when I was born decades ago?"

Louve said it with a sarcastic tone that made Carmine half-irritated, half-embarrassed, but she had a point. More than her name, Carmine wanted to know the woman's nature. So she asked, "*What* are you?"

"Like you said," Louve answered, slowly walking toward Carmine, looking completely unabashed. "I'm a she-wolf. A dream-walker—though I only walk the dreams of my own kind."

"But you are human, too."

"I am, but I rarely wander in this form these days." She paused, examining Carmine before adding, "Those who know about our existence call us dream-walkers indeed, but we ourselves prefer the word lycanthropes."

Lycanthropes. Carmine stood still, absorbing the information, analyzing the word, almost savoring it. Then she looked Louve in the eye and told her, "You said you can only walk the dreams of your kind, yet you walked *my* dreams."

"I assume your husband wasn't very helpful, if that surprises you."

"He admitted lying to me," Carmine responded, clenching her fists, "but he refused to say about what. All I know is that my spell is more than my grandmother said it was, and that it was preventing you and other dream—other *lycanthropes*—from walking my dreams."

Louve nodded. "You aren't a lycanthrope, but you could be if you chose to. That's why I can walk your dreams." She was close to Carmine now and extended her hand in a peaceful gesture. "We didn't start on the right foot, you and I. The first time I saw you, you had just killed my friend." She glanced at the grave. "His name was Ronan, and he was a lycanthrope too. I had told him many times not to approach your village in his wolf form, but he didn't listen, and that fool even killed your sheep. That's why you came to hunt him. You didn't know what he was, that he was your moon-brother, because you didn't even know what *you* were. I understood it after your mind became visible to me for the first time during the following full moon."

Louve continued to offer her hand to Carmine, who didn't know what to do about it. The feelings inside of her fought each other, and none were at the point of emerging victorious over the others. Anger, fear, excitement, everything melted into a pool of confusion that drowned her mind into paralysis. She wanted to know *everything*, but she was also scared of the answers she would get. And even though she discovered that she couldn't trust her husband, that didn't mean she should trust Louve blindly.

"Carmine," Louve said gently, her voice silvery and her somber eyes riveted on Carmine's. "Let's talk."

Hearing her name inside Louve's mouth sent a shiver down her spine, snapping Carmine out of her emotional stupor. She didn't take Louve's hand, but she followed her to the grave. The cold was harrowing, and she wondered how Louve wasn't freezing to death with her skin exposed to the elements. Was it because she was a lycanthrope? As if Louve had heard her thoughts, she changed into her wolf form. Her body reshaped its arms and legs into four smaller, but more powerful limbs. Brown fur grew from her pale skin, and her dark eyes became amber. Carmine gasped in surprise, enthralled by how a human body could undergo such a dramatic change in only an instant. It had been so sudden and smooth, as if Louve had slipped inside a wolf's skin between two steps.

"My apologies for the unexpected shift," she said, "but I was getting cold and didn't need my hands anymore. Sit."

Carmine hesitated, but eventually did as she was told and sat on the grassy ground next to Louve. She couldn't help but stare at Louve's powerful jaw, where the teeth that had tried to snap her neck not so long ago hid. Would she have spared the sheep-killing wolf—Ronan—if she had known he wasn't a mere animal? Or would she have killed him all the same, seeing him as an abomination threatening the village? Common folks accepted witchcraft because witches helped improve their livelihood with potions and spells, but lycanthropes would certainly stir fear and disgust inside the villagers' hearts. Inside Carmine's heart, too, if curiosity and awe hadn't filled it first upon meeting Louve.

"You said I could become a lycanthrope," Carmine said. "Why?"

Louve snorted, revealing her deadly white fangs. "Aren't you more interested in the *how*?"

Carmine didn't reply immediately. Louve had just offered to tell her how to gain the ability to turn into one of the beasts she has been hunting for the last decade. To become the enemy. Now she understood why Dacien hadn't wanted to tell her, because the promise of gaining such power was both revolting and horribly tempting. Still, it didn't justify his refusal to tell her the truth.

"I would like to know both," she admitted at last.

"Fair enough," Louve said. "Like me and other lycanthropes, you are moon-marked. This simply means you were born during the fourth full moon of the season."

Carmine blinked. "I can become a lycanthrope only because of *when* I was born?"

"Yes. It can happen to anyone. The poor and the aristocrat, the virtuous and the wicked. The moon claims us blindly. Most people don't know about it, and the parents aren't aware of their child's potential."

"But my grandmother—"

"Was a witch. She knew. Your parents knew." Louve paused, then added, stating the obvious that had already manifested itself into Carmine's mind, "They hid the truth from you."

Carmine gritted her teeth. So it wasn't only Dacien who lied. Her parents. Her grandmother. *Was I the only one unaware of my own nature?* she thought bitterly.

She exhaled slowly, trying to calm her racing thoughts, then asked, "What about the *how*, then?"

Louve's serious expression turned amused, satisfaction evident in her voice as she said, "Now we are talking. There's only one way for the moon-marked to awaken their lycanthropy."

She paused, as if waiting for Carmine to say something. But Carmine stared at Louve apprehensively, silent, eager to learn more. Now that Louve had begun, Carmine couldn't wait to hear it, so she nodded at Louve to encourage her to continue.

"When a moon-marked reaches puberty," Louve finally said, "other lycanthropes can start walking into their dreams and form bonds with them. When they're ready, the moon-marked will lie with another lycanthrope of their choice to awaken their powers."

Carmine blinked, suddenly understanding where the conversation was going. "Must the moon-marked... consent?"

"No," Louve said. "The moon doesn't care if your lycanthropy is awakened of your own free-will or by force."

"So your cousin who attacked me ten years ago was trying to... awaken it?"

"Obviously," Louve said. "He got what he deserved for trying to force himself on you. I'm glad your husband eliminated him. No one misses that swine."

Carmine clenched her fists as she remembered the big bad wolf's uncanny smile and ravenous look. She was glad he was dead. Not only had he tried to rape her, but he would have taken her free will away, forcing her to become a lycanthrope. At fourteen years old. How would her life be if she had gained the ability to turn into a wolf ten years ago, before she had enough control over her emotions and actions? Surely the young girl that she was then wouldn't have controlled her shifting. She would have been ostracized by other villagers, forced to live in the forest as a beast or to journey to another village far enough from Ozaryn that her reputation wouldn't follow her. Was that why Louve and Ronan lived in a den in the woods? Or had they chosen this recluse life?

"Why do you live in the forest, Louve?" she asked.

Louve's pupils narrowed and her ears flipped back, giving her a happily surprised look. "I like it," she replied with a honeyed voice, as if tasting her own words.

"Is that true?"

"It wasn't always the case," Louve conceded after a brief silence. "At first, I had no other choice. My own parents threatened to chase me away after I told them I wanted to awaken my lycanthropy with the help of another lycanthrope I had feelings for. She had been visiting my dreams for years and after I met her in person, I knew she would be the one to take my maidenhood. But my parents never understood the dreams, the calling, the magic, the bond between a lycanthrope and their moon-marked maiden, no matter how much I explained it to them. They wanted me to preserve myself and my humanity so I could marry some son of a rich merchant, while my cousin was already running wild into the woods. So at seventeen, I disobeyed, lay with my then-partner, and learned to shift. I came back home to my family, told them what I had done, and the next day I was gone, dead to them."

"I'm sorry," Carmine whispered.

"Don't be," Louve said. "I knew what to expect. It was a rash decision, but I chose it. And you should be able to choose, too."

An uncomfortable but alluring thought crossed Carmine's mind. Could she awaken her lycanthropy... with Louve? She had seen her human body, and she wouldn't be against getting a closer taste of it. Louve was as attractive as a wolf's heart had once been to Carmine's arrows. But before she could entertain the idea further, or even—if she dared—*ask* Louve, the lycanthrope said, "I don't know if you can, though. Your spell doesn't protect you from dream-walking anymore, but it might still prevent you from awakening your lycanthropy."

Carmine sighed. It was probably true. Anyway, she didn't know if she wanted to awaken her lycanthropy or not. She had hated wolves since the big bad wolf had tried to eat—no, to *rape* her and *awaken* her lycanthropy, dear heavens. She had married a hunter. Had mastered the hunting arts herself, and built her entire livelihood out of wolf hunting. And now she was considering becoming a lycanthrope? How could she throw her entire life out of the window like that? But looking at Louve... she couldn't help but feel envious. Carmine had more freedom than other women in her village because she was a huntress and childless, but how long would that last? She would find herself with child eventually, and Dacien wouldn't let her hunt anymore. He had promised it would be temporary, but what if she became pregnant again? And again? Soon hunting would have no more place in her existence. Meanwhile, Louve had given up her old life so she could run free in the forest alongside her then-partner. She could hunt as much as she wanted—she simply hunted a different type of prey. Could Carmine be self-fulfilled by hunting not as a human, but as a wolf?

She shook her head, trying to chase the conflicting thoughts away, and said, "I don't know if I want it."

"To choose?"

"No. To become a lycanthrope."

Louve nodded. "You should be the master of your own destiny, Carmine. Not my cousin, not your grandmother, not your husband. It doesn't matter what you do in the end."

Chapter Ten

Now

Louve's words sunk into Carmine's mind. *It doesn't matter what you do in the end.* She was right. Whether Carmine became a lycanthrope or not, what mattered was that she got to decide *herself*.

As she readied herself to leave the forest that could become her new home, Carmine finally took the hand Louve offered to her.

"Thank you for speaking with me," she told the lycanthrope. She almost said *for being truthful*, but Carmine wanted to confirm Louve's words before trusting her fully.

"I'll wait for you," Louve said. "Whatever you decide, please come find me once you have freed yourself."

Carmine nodded silently, resisting the urge to touch more than Louve's hand, and left.

She knew only one person who could confirm or deny Louve's assertions—and it wasn't Dacien, since he had sworn not to say a thing and wasn't willing to break his oath. Another witch. Ezélise, her great-aunt. But first, she wanted to see for herself that the big bad wolf had indeed been a lycanthrope like Louve and Ronan. If this was true, he would have reverted to his original form in death, leaving behind human bones like Ronan. She only needed to convince Dacien to tell her where he had buried the remains. For that, she was ready to fill his ears with sweet words and half-lies.

Carmine knocked on the door of her own home. Dacien opened it and looked at her with wide eyes, before saying, "Finally, you're back." She didn't answer, so he continued, "You have to stop running away without warning. I won't be able to help you if you get into trouble and I don't know where you are."

She gave him a faint smile and nodded. "I'm sorry for causing you to worry. I just needed some fresh air to think about what we discussed. May I come in?"

He let her in, then he asked, "So, did the outdoors help clear your mind?"

"It did," she said, keeping *but not as you expected* to herself. "I'm sorry for my recent behavior. The attack of the she-wolf opened up some old wounds that I thought had healed. I was wrong to believe I was strong enough not to be disturbed by it. I need to heal for good and put my past behind me."

"I'm glad to hear it," Dacien said, letting out a sigh of relief. After a brief pause, he added, "I shouldn't have let you go hunting alone. We're partners. We should have waited for me to come back from my other hunt to complete this contract together."

"What is done is done," Carmine said very fast. "Don't blame yourself. We both agreed to me taking the contract alone. This won't happen again."

"Good."

"Also..." Carmine added, averting her gaze. "I thought about the spell."

Dacien's face hardened, as if he was anticipating another argument.

"You don't have to tell me if you want to keep your oath to my grandmother," she said softly, ignoring the lump in her throat and her angry thoughts. "I trust you. If you think I need to get it fixed so it can protect me from wolves and dreams, I'll have it done. I will visit Aunt Ezélise. I don't like her, but she'll know what to do."

For an instant, Carmine feared Dacien wouldn't believe her feigned change of heart, but to her relief, his face softened. He looked her in the eye and said, "Thank you. I swear this is truly for the best."

"I believe you." She looked down, worried that he could see her true thoughts if he looked too long into the window to her soul. He had known her for a long time. She had lied to him in the past, but always about inconsequential things. Steeling her heart, she looked up again and said, "You never told me where you buried the wolf."

He frowned. "I buried it close to your grandmother's house. Why?"

"I think it would make me feel better if I stopped by it on my way to Aunt Ezélise's. Perhaps it would give me some closure if I saw it. I know it's dead, but sometimes I feel like a part of my mind is still... afraid. Seeing the grave could make it real for good."

He inhaled deeply, hesitating for a moment, but at last he said, "Perhaps it would do you some good, yes. But I didn't mark the grave. The beast didn't deserve it."

That she agreed with wholeheartedly, and didn't have to pretend when she replied, "You did right. It deserves to be forgotten.

Hopefully, I'll be able to fully put its memory behind me after I see its resting place, and no one will remember it, not even myself."

He nodded. "We could go together. I didn't mark the grave, but I know where it is."

"No, I need to do this alone. This is between me and my past."

Carmine held her breath as she waited for his answer, scared he would refuse to let her go without him. Finally he said, "I buried it at the foot of the old weeping willow in your grandmother's garden, on the north side."

She knew exactly where that was, but an herbalist had purchased her grandmother's house after her passing. Carmine's parents had no use for the red-bricked house in Alverton, and they had welcomed the money, as work had become more difficult over the past years with old age.

I'll find a way, she reassured herself. And even if she couldn't see the human bones by herself, she would still visit Aunt Ezélise and get answers. Aunt Ezélise disliked Carmine's grandmother as much as Carmine's grandmother had disliked Aunt Ezélise. If Aunt Ezélise knew something about lycanthropes and the spell, she would likely delight in telling Carmine everything her grandmother had not wanted her to know, if only to spite her sister's memory and ruin the love Carmine had for her—not that much of it remained inside Carmine's heart.

The next morning, Carmine packed enough supplies for a three-day walk and put on a hooded cloak to keep herself warm. As she was about to leave, Dacien handed Carmine her bow, quiver, and hunting knives.

"So nobody dares bothering you during your journey," he said, before embracing her.

Strange feelings filled Carmine's heart as she felt Dacien's body against hers. He was saying goodbye, expecting to see her in a week, when she didn't know if she would ever come back. Even if she did, things would never be the same between them. She had dearly loved him, once. Or at least she thought she had. They had grown close after he had started training her, and shortly after she had turned seventeen, he had proposed to her and they had exchanged their first kiss. She still remembered it after all these years, but the butterflies she once felt in her stomach had long flown away.

She didn't hate her husband. Anger and disappointment filled her mind and fueled her determination, but she didn't have the resolve to harbor heavy feelings toward him. Carmine wanted to be free to carve her own destiny and move on without being burdened by her past—and she felt in her bones that soon her husband would join it. So she embraced him too, saying farewell not with words but with a tight, affectionate clasp, before leaving the place that she had called home for years, but that felt foreign already.

The icy wind blew hard against Carmine's cheeks as she walked to Alverton, announcing a rigid winter that would soon descend upon the region. Soon the land would become white and silent, and soon Carmine would roam it unbound, without spells stopping her from choosing her path.

Carmine found the red-bricked house unchanged, still standing on the town's western border. She pulled her hood back and knocked on the door. The herbalist—a short woman with curly blond hair and a pointed chin—opened it and said, "You're the former owner's granddaughter."

"Ezilda was my grandmother, yes," Carmine said, politely bowing her head.

"Come in," the herbalist said. "It's freezing outside."

"Thank you, but I'm not here to buy."

"It's still freezing outside. Come in, I said."

Carmine opened her mouth to argue, but the herbalist pulled her inside the shop before she could speak. Inside, a strong smell of sage mixed with burning wood assaulted her senses. She hadn't intended to impose herself inside the herbalist's shop, but she was thankful for the quick break from the elements.

As the herbalist poured thyme tea inside a brownish ceramic cup, Carmine said, "I won't stay long."

"Traveling for some big game hunt, aren't you?"

"I—yes, exactly."

"Where is it taking you?"

"To Céracuse," she said, not really lying, as she had named the closest village to Aunt Ezélise's cabin.

"That's quite the walk you have," the herbalist said. "Hope you don't plan to stop by your grandmother's sister's place." Carmine shook her head, ignoring her clenching heart and dry mouth. "That old hag still owes me a tidy sum of money for supplies I delivered more than six months ago. She keeps stealing from honest folks and doing the moon-knows-what, that sad witch. Should have listened to your grandmother when she told me not to deal with her. I guess I can only blame myself."

Nodding quietly, Carmine brought the teacup to her lips and drank a couple of gulps before putting it down. She enjoyed the herbalist's hospitality, but had a long journey ahead of her and was itching to search for the big bad wolf's remains—though she didn't know how to breach the topic without sounding rude.

To her relief, the herbalist said, "So what brings you here if you won't buy any of my supplies? I suppose you didn't stop to sip some tea."

"It's going to sound odd," Carmine answered, "but I hoped to see the old weeping willow in your garden. My grandmother and I used to sit under it when I was a little girl, and I have fond memories of our time there."

"Missing your grandmother, are you? She was a good witch, the old lady. Often bought my supplies—and always paid on time, mind you."

Carmine nodded. "She also enchanted the tree so it would make me feel better when she sang my favorite rhyme under it." She told the story she had come up with while walking to Alverton. "The hunt awaiting me in Céracuse will be challenging, and I need all the help I can get."

"So you want me to let you go sing under the weeping willow?"

Carmine nodded again. "If you don't mind, of course. I don't want to intrude. I'll be on my way if you prefer me not to go into your garden."

"I let you inside my shop to drink some tea. I can let you perform some harmless witchy ritual under my weeping willow. It *is* harmless, right? You aren't going to cast a spell yourself or something of that sort, are you?"

The herbalist winked at Carmine, who gave her a strained smile before saying, "Completely harmless. Thank you." She kept her rebuttal of the herbalist's insinuation to herself. There had once been rumors about Carmine's grandmother training her into witchcraft, but they had ceased after Dacien took Carmine under his wing to make a huntress out of her. It seemed some people still believed it—the herbalist one of them, and Carmine couldn't blame her. Once, it had been a tradition for witches and druids to train their grandchildren in their arts, should they manifest a predisposition for learning magic. But Carmine had never been interested in witchcraft beyond a natural child's curiosity, and now she wondered if her grandmother would have accepted her as an apprentice since she was moon-marked. *Probably not,* Carmine told herself, aptly remembering how her grandmother had never offered to teach her witchcraft.

The herbalist walked her to the back of the house and opened the door to the garden. There, in the middle of the grass, was the venerable tree next to which Dacien had buried a wolf carcass that should now be human bones. While lycanthropes shifted between their human and lupine forms in the blink of an eye, the reversal to their original form took many hours in death, Louve had told Carmine. Dacien had probably not seen it and buried the body while it was still covered in fur, meaning the big bad wolf must have become human again in the ground. This guaranteed a decayed and deformed body no one would wish to see, but Carmine was determined to confirm Louve's story with her own eyes.

She waited for the herbalist to retreat inside her home before she started digging with her bare hands. At that moment, she wished she was a lycanthrope, for she could have become a wolf and removed the ground much faster with paws. Instead, she could barely feel her cold, numb fingers as she broke her nails against the icy dirt. Glancing over her shoulder to check if the herbalist was still inside, she kept digging and digging until she hit something hard. She held her breath as she uncovered a long bone—a femur way too big to belong to a wolf.

"What are you doing?"

Carmine froze as she heard the herbalist's question.

"I said, what are you doing?"

The voice was closer now, and angrier. Quickly, Carmine covered her deathly findings with dirt. She didn't want to explain why a corpse was buried in the garden, or why she had been digging it up. Then she rose and turned, locking eyes with the herbalist, who looked furious.

"What wicked witchcraft is that?" she asked, glancing at Carmine's dirt-covered fingers. "You said you were going to *sing*, not dig into my garden. Are you burying a spell-stone to curse me? You want the house back? Your mother regrets selling it to me? She's not happy with the exorbitant amount of money she got from me? What is it? Speak!"

Carmine didn't respond and kept staring at the herbalist, unable to choose an appropriate answer among the dozens of excuses racing through her mind. The herbalist relentlessly questioned her as she stalked closer. Soon she would be within grasp.

At last, Carmine reacted and said very fast, "I have to go."

"You're not going anywhere. You're going to follow me to the mayor's house and we're going to sort this out the right way. I'm tired of letting your family swindle me after being so nice to all of you."

No, I'm not following you anywhere, pushed itself to the front of Carmine's mind. She knew she had to leave. Either by running and jumping above the fence, hoping she would be fast enough to climb it before the herbalist reached her, or by using one of her hunting knives to intimidate the woman. She had never used a knife against a human—*not knowingly,* she told herself as she remembered hurting Ronan and Louve in their wolf forms—and she didn't feel like starting today. So she inhaled deeply and sprinted toward the fence, silently praying not to slip and fall.

Thankfully, it hadn't rained or snowed yet, and the wood was dry and easy to climb for someone agile like Carmine. Behind her, the herbalist cursed, swearing not to let the matter go.

"You're not welcome in Alverton anymore, you filthy whore," the herbalist shouted as Carmine let herself fall to the other side of the fence, finally free.

Ignoring the curious looks from the villagers, she dashed through the town, her mind solely focused on leaving Alverton as quickly as possible and pursuing her journey toward Céracuse. Once she reached the eastern border of the town and beyond, the much-desired path of solitude until the next town, she allowed herself to think about what she had found under the weeping willow. She had only caught a glimpse of the bone before the herbalist interrupted her, but she was sure. It was too thick and too long to belong to a wolf, and if the corpse belonged to the big bad wolf like Dacien had told her, then she couldn't allow herself to doubt anymore. The wicked beast that had tricked her ten years ago truly was a lycanthrope like Louve, and not an enchanted animal like her grandmother had pretended.

She kept running but slowed down her pace once she was far enough from Alverton, her loaded backpack feeling heavy on her shoulders after the burst of effort she had executed. What had happened in the herbalist's garden would soon spread across the region, and Dacien would hear about it. Her parents, too, though the thought of her mother being embarrassed by the news didn't bother Carmine. After all, it was her mother who had sent her to Alverton when she was only fourteen, pretending she had to bring medicine to her not-so-sick grandmother. It had been a stratagem to make her visit the old woman, so she would ink the spell on her back. Carmine didn't believe her mother had planned for the big bad wolf to attack her, but if she had told her the truth, none of that would have happened. Carmine would have never told the wolf where she was going. She would have been better prepared. By sending Carmine to Alverton alone after she had reached menarche, her mother had sent her right into the wolf's den.

Would she really be unwelcome in Alverton as the herbalist had promised? And what about Ozaryn? How would the townspeople react after hearing the herbalist's accusations? Dacien could dispel them, of course. He knew what lay under the weeping willow, and that

Carmine wasn't a witch planting spell-stones. People would realize it had all been a big misunderstanding. But... the herbalist was probably already digging under the tree, and she would find the bones. Then she would accuse Carmine's family of murdering and burying someone in the garden, and tell everyone she could. Dacien would also ask Carmine why she dug out the bones, and wouldn't appreciate her answer. The more she thought about it, the more difficult it became to find excuses to justify her behavior if she wished to resume her previous life after removing the spell from her back. Not that she had planned on going back to normal—she still wasn't sure—but her actions were deciding for her.

Carmine spent the rest of the day dwelling on the consequences of her actions until her mind became numb and tired. Shortly before the sun set, she stopped at an inn at the crossroads of major trading routes and booked a room for the night. Because she had been running instead of walking, she had covered more ground than expected. If she traveled at the same pace the next day, she would reach Aunt Ezélise's place before sundown. For that, she would need a good night of sleep, and she worried her preoccupied mind wouldn't let her have it. She wished the moon was full again, so Louve could visit her dreams and perhaps ease her sleep, but dark clouds hid a gibbous moon that wouldn't be full for several weeks.

She still dreamt of Louve, and of what they could do together to awaken Carmine's lycanthropy.

Chapter Eleven

Now

Carmine woke up at dawn, feeling only half-refreshed by the night. At least her backpack was lighter as she had eaten through her supplies, allowing her to keep a steady pace on the road. Dozens of merchants greeted Carmine on her way to Céracuse, distracting her mind from the past day's events in Alverton. But as she got closer to her destination, she felt a knot in her stomach. Carmine hadn't seen her great-aunt for years. Would Aunt Ezélise agree to help her, despite the harsh words Carmine had spat at her during their last encounter? The last time she had seen Aunt Ezélise was in Alverton alongside her grandmother, and the two sisters had bickered for what felt like hours until Carmine had put an end to the conflict by siding with her grandmother and telling Aunt Ezélise to go back into her forsaken hole in the forest. She couldn't remember what the disagreement had been about, but she clearly remembered—her cheeks warming with embarrassment at the memory—Aunt Ezélise's vexed face and black look. She would understand if Aunt Ezélise was still mad at her, unwilling to accept her humblest apologies.

The sky was sunless when she reached the woods where Aunt Ezélise lived. No road led to her place, not even a narrow path among the trees. Carmine would have to rely on her memory to find the place, and she could barely recall a single detail from her last visit. Gathering her courage, she left the safety of the road and stepped inside the forest to search for Aunt Ezélise's cabin.

She looked for an hour or two, perhaps more. Each time she found a cabin, her heartbeat quickened until she walked closer and realized it was either a seasonal hunter lodge or an abandoned hut, and not Aunt Ezélise's home. What if the witch didn't live here anymore, and Carmine was wandering the woods for nothing? What if her great-aunt was *dead*, and she didn't even know? Aunt Ezélise was younger than Carmine's grandmother, but she was still old and closer to death with each passing day. Common superstition pretended witches lived longer than regular folks, but that wasn't true. No potion or spell could slow down aging, and even if magic helped witches and their clients cure diseases and heal injuries, time claimed everyone in the end.

Unable to see the stars, Carmine lost track of time. She was about to succumb to despair—she would never find her great-aunt!—when a familiar voice said, "What are you doing, silly girl?"

Carmine would have smiled if she wasn't so tense. She turned to Aunt Ezélise and found the witch wearing a cloak similar to her own, except it was gray and not red. Her wrinkled face and sparkling eyes showed a blend of curiosity and amusement, and not an ounce of hostility.

"Looking for you, of course," Carmine said, relieved.

Aunt Ezélise let out a teasing laugh. "And doing so in the dead of night, going in circles like an aimless fool."

"Well, it worked. I found you."

"Or rather, *I* found you. You've been making such a racket. I had to investigate."

Carmine stifled a snort. She had been quiet, walking carefully as if she was stalking prey, but Aunt Ezélise wasn't a mere old woman living in the woods. She used magic to sharpen her senses, and could hear and see far beyond normal reach. Druids manipulated magic to enhance their own bodies to better commune with the wilderness they lived in, something witchcraft couldn't achieve. This had led Carmine's grandmother to suspect her sister had mingled with druids and learned their ways, giving her one more reason to dislike Ezélise.

"So what brings you to my forsaken hole, hmm?" Aunt Ezélise asked as she escorted Carmine to her place.

Carmine winced. "You remember."

"Of course I remember," Aunt Ezélise replied. "Do you think I'm senile?"

"No, no... it was a long time ago, and I just hoped—"

"That I would have forgotten or forgiven you for parroting everything my sister said about me?"

Carmine exhaled. "Listen, I'm sorry. I shouldn't have spoken to you so rudely. You're right. I was... young, and influenced by my grandmother. I loved and trusted her. Blindly. If she said your witchcraft was bad, I would believe her, no questions asked."

Aunt Ezélise gave her a half-satisfied, half-mocking smile, before saying, "Forgotten, I have not, but forgiving you? I guess I can do that.

It was indeed a long time ago. It looks like your grandmother's absence has allowed you to grow your own mind."

The merciful words warmed Carmine's heart, reassuring her. "More than I expected," she admitted.

Aunt Ezélise nodded, and they kept walking in a comfortable silence until they reached their destination. Carmine suspected her great-aunt used witchcraft to hide her cabin, because she could swear that she had crossed the clearing it was located in without seeing it.

The place had changed a lot since the last time Carmine had visited. She didn't remember much about the exterior of the house, but she remembered its inside: a bright, lively place with a lot of sunlight and colorful pots, figurines, and herbs hanging on the walls. Now the curtains were all closed, plunging the place into darkness, and the walls were devoid of ornaments. Carmine didn't know why, but it looked like Aunt Ezélise had lost interest in leading a cheerful life. Was this what happened when someone became plagued by old age? Or had something specific ruined her great-aunt's mood for good? Too polite to ask, Carmine didn't say a word and followed Aunt Ezélise near the hearth.

"You didn't answer my question," the witch said. "Why did you travel all this way by yourself to see me?"

Carmine removed her jacket, her hands slightly trembling. "It might be easier to show you rather than going into the lengthy explanation."

She stood in silence, showing her back to her great-aunt, bracing herself for a conversation she was both eager and scared to have. What if her great-aunt couldn't help her?

Aunt Ezélise whispered a short incantation that illuminated the air around them, then she looked at the damaged tattoo and exclaimed, "By the moon!"

"My grandmother told me it was a mere protection spell against wolves," Carmine began, "but I recently learned that—"

"That you're moon-marked and it's preventing you from awakening your powers, right?"

"Yes," Carmine said, shocked by the plain tone Aunt Ezélise used, as if she was talking about the weather. Her great-aunt couldn't think being a lycanthrope was such an anecdotal thing, could she? But to Carmine's relief, Aunt Ezélise confirmed it was true, giving her the definitive answer she wanted. "She lied to me about so many things."

Aunt Ezélise clicked her tongue. "I know it's bad to curse the dead, but she was a wench for doing that to you. Tattooing a spell without telling you what it really does."

Carmine nodded in silence. She agreed with her great-aunt, but didn't want to badmouth her grandmother. Despite what she had learned over the last few days, she had fond memories of their time together, and couldn't resolve to insult her.

"Did you know I was moon-marked at birth?"

"Of course I knew," Aunt Ezélise said, rolling her eyes. "Do you think I'm that mediocre? I wasn't there, but I saw you a few days after you were born. When Ezilda told me your date of birth, I told her she had to help you."

"Help me?"

Aunt Ezélise exhaled, her mouth twisting into a sympathetic smile. She said softly, almost whispering, "Tell you what it means to be moon-marked. Give you options. Perhaps even find another dream-walker to tell you about shifting and dream-walking. The usual. So it's not a surprise when it happens, and you can decide what to do about your gift. Keep it dormant with a spell like this one"—she pointed at Carmine's back—"if that's your wish, or awaken it. But she didn't listen and thought she knew what was good for you."

Tears came to Carmine's eyes, but she managed to prevent them from rolling down her cheeks. How heartbreaking was it to hear these pleasant, much-wanted words not from the mouth of the grandmother she had loved, but from the great-aunt she had unfairly distrusted! She wanted to ask Aunt Ezélise why she hadn't told her, but she could guess her reasons to remain quiet. Carmine's grandmother must have threatened to retaliate if she told her, and Carmine herself didn't give many reasons to Aunt Ezélise to be kind to her once she grew up and started repeating the slander her grandmother had fed her.

"You silly girl," Aunt Ezélise said after noticing Carmine's wet eyes. "Come here."

Aunt Ezélise opened her arms, inviting Carmine to join her for a comforting embrace. Carmine hesitated for barely a second before nestling against her great-aunt and freeing the tears she had been holding back. She cried silently, unable to find the words to express her feelings. Disappointment. Sadness. Regret. Her entire life would have been different if her grandmother had listened to her sister.

"I know," Aunt Ezélise whispered a couple of times while gently hugging Carmine, as if she could read her mind.

Once Carmine had calmed down and her cheeks had gone dry, Aunt Ezélise looked again at the magical tattoo on her back. "This is a complex spell," she said. "I see multiple enchantments in these lines. The ones forming the spell to repel dream-walkers' nightly intrusions have been seriously damaged"—she touched Carmine's skin where Louve had sunk in her claws and left large, still-visible scars—"as well as the lines forming the mere wolf-repelling magic. She didn't lie when she said the spell was protecting you from wolves, but it was obviously doing a lot more."

"What about the part that seals my powers away? That prevents me from awakening even if I… if I lie with another one."

"It's mostly intact. There's one line that has been a little damaged, but probably not enough to break the spell entirely."

"Can you break it?" Carmine asked eagerly.

Aunt Ezélise shrugged. "Yes. I can fix the tattoo, or I can break the remaining spells if you want."

"Spells? There are more?"

"I see one more," Aunt Ezélise said, running her finger on Carmine's back. "I'm not sure what this is, but these lines aren't a part of the three other spells, and they can't be here only for aesthetic purposes."

Carmine frowned. Another spell? Did Louve omit to mention another power lycanthropes had that the fourth spell sealed away? But Aunt Ezélise would know about it and wouldn't sound so confused about it. What could it be, then? A spell to bind her to Dacien, perhaps? Was their marriage tainted with foul magic? What *else* had her grandmother taken away from Carmine without telling her?

Aunt Ezélise fetched a bulky grimoire and browsed through the pages until she stopped and gasped. "I can't believe it," she whispered angrily, before showing the grimoire to Carmine. Above a complex pattern was written the name of the spell: *infertility*.

Carmine's eyes opened wide as all the pieces of her life fell together into one coherent picture. Her grandmother was responsible for her lack of pregnancy after all these years trying! Did Dacien know about that part of the magical tattoo, too? *No, he didn't,* she told herself. He had always been genuine in his desire to become a father. And though motherhood had never appealed to Carmine, knowing that she had been deprived of it not by choice, but by malice, was infuriating.

"Why?" was the only question that escaped her lips. Carmine could fathom why her grandmother had prevented her from becoming a lycanthrope, but infertility? She couldn't understand.

"There are some far-fetched theories about dream-walking being inheritable," Aunt Ezélise said. "I assume your grandmother worried you could give birth to another future dream-walker, even without becoming one yourself."

"But I thought it was related to the moon and your time of birth," Carmine said bitterly, her voice raising as if she was arguing with her dead grandmother.

"I know, I know," Aunt Ezélise said pressingly, putting a comforting hand on Carmine's shoulder. "I don't believe in the inheritable theory. But I know some witches do, and they advise moon-marked not to conceive children, so they don't pass on their gift—or rather, their *curse,* according to them. It's pure superstition, if you ask me, and I would have never imagined Ezilda to believe in it. But I don't see why she would have put that spell on you if not because of that foolish theory."

"Remove it," Carmine said firmly. She was done letting a tattoo and its enchanted ink dictate what she could do with her life. She was done pondering her options.

"What about the other spells?"

She didn't hesitate before responding, her voice quavering yet assertive, "Remove *all of them.*"

"It's going to hurt," Aunt Ezélise warned. "The only way to remove the spells is to break enough critical lines on your skin."

"Can't you use a spell to remove the enchanted ink?"

Aunt Ezélise shook her head. "No. I will have to break the lines the same way the others were broken. But I will make precise, small incisions to limit the pain, and I will heal your wounds the best I can afterwards."

Carmine gritted her teeth, but her will didn't bend despite the painful procedure awaiting her. She handed one of her own hunting knives to Aunt Ezélise and said, "Do it."

Nodding silently, Aunt Ezélise took the knife. As Carmine readied herself for the blade, she thought of Louve. Of her jet-black hair falling over her breasts, and her night-like eyes that Carmine couldn't wait to drown in.

Then she screamed.

Epilogue

Carmine found Louve at dusk in the clearing where she had last seen her. As promised, she had waited for her. She wore a long fur cloak neatly tightened around her naked shoulders and light leather shoes that left oval footprints in the nascent snow. The rest of her body was bare and protected from the elements solely by the buttoned cloak.

"It's done," Carmine said as Louve lay eyes on her.

Louve nodded silently, then offered her hand to Carmine. Without hesitating, Carmine took it, and followed Louve deeper into the woods.

"Have you chosen your path?" Louve asked.

Carmine tightened her fingers around Louve's hand and said, "I have."

"So this is farewell, I guess?" Louve said, glancing at Carmine's hunting attire. "You're going back to him."

Carmine gave her a soft smile and said, "No, this is not."

She was indeed dressed as if she was going back home to reunite with her husband and go on another hunt—and to be truthful, she hoped to see him again. Not today, not tomorrow, but eventually, Carmine would go back to Ozaryn. She had thought about it for a long time while walking back to the clearing. Dacien had lied to her, but the real culprit was dead and had, to some extent, deceived him too. Aunt Ezélise's revelation about the infertility spell didn't absolve Dacien of his other sins, but had somewhat softened Carmine's anger toward him. She wasn't ready yet, but perhaps she would find the strength to forgive him one day, should he demonstrate genuine regret for lying to her. Perhaps they could still have a future together, and if Carmine chose it, children. But she wouldn't go back to Dacien as her old self. She would choose her own path here, now, with Louve. Soon her home wouldn't be limited to four walls, or her love to one person.

Turning to Louve, Carmine leaned over and gently kissed her. Her lips were soft and cold like frost, but soon they warmed under Carmine's tender touch. Louve moved back, a look of surprise on her face. After a second that felt like tormenting hours, she smiled and pressed her body and her lips against Carmine's, resuming what shouldn't have been interrupted.

Carmine felt warm inside, as if Louve was pouring hot sunlight directly into her soul. Never before had she been enchanted like this by a simple kiss. But the scathing, icy air was stronger than Louve's warmth, and soon Carmine began shaking. Louve, too, looked like she was suffering from the cold under her cloak. Goosebumps covered her body, and though Carmine was certain that Louve felt as warm as herself inside, she doubted that her skin was only reacting to her feelings.

"Come," Louve said after ending their embrace. "Let's get warmer."

Carmine gulped, wondering if Louve meant the words literally, or in a different manner. She realized Louve meant both when they reached a small cabin with a wood fire burning out front. Around the fire were spread two large bear pelts. Carmine wondered if that was where Louve spent the night in her wolf form, the fire protecting her from the cold and other predators, and if she used the cabin when she needed to look human. But she didn't ask, and lay next to Louve on one of the soft brown pelts. The fire brought enough warmth for Carmine to feel comfortable removing her clothes, which she did with Louve's help.

"Are you sure about this?" Louve asked while glancing at Carmine's naked body. "Once it awakens, it can't become dormant again."

Carmine had never been so sure, so she nodded. "I'll always be able to choose when to shift and when to walk another lycanthrope's dreams, right?"

"You will—though I'll visit your dreams if you don't visit mine, maiden," Louve said, grinning.

Carmine grinned back, and Louve dropped a gentle kiss on her lips before she showed Carmine how a lycanthrope awoke another's powers. Carmine looked back and forth between the sky, where the half-moon shone high and bright, and Louve. At first, she found herself struggling to let go and enjoy Louve's delicate lips and tongue on her flesh, but soon she realized Louve was too dedicated not to feel overwhelmed with a pleasure she would die of if she did not externalize it. So she moaned and ran her fingers through Louve's lush, silken hair to guide her—though Louve didn't need any guiding, and devoured Carmine with fervent perfection, as if she already knew every inch of her body.

Carmine wished it would have lasted forever, but soon a heavenly and uncontainable wave of pleasure seized her. Carmine let out a loud, unrestrained moan before shouting her lover's name in an ecstatic plea. When she looked down at her, Louve had a satisfied smile on her face. As Carmine kissed Louve's wet lips, she noticed the intense warmth that had filled her body with blissfulness was still there, but it felt different. It was as if something vital and profound had revealed itself inside her.

Louve whispered into her ear, "Try it."

A shiver rippled down Carmine's spine, but she nodded. Then she shifted, the transformation exquisitely effortless as if she had always been able to do so. She felt her body and mind explode with primal joy as thick gray fur grew on her skin for the first time.

She looked up at the moon, and howled.

Acknowledgements

Special thanks to the following people for their unending support and friendship:

My spouse, Félix, for calling this story *weird*, which is always a compliment when said about my writing.

My cover artist, Ruth Anna, who not only designed the pretty cover but also convinced me to keep submitting this story to publishers until it found its home.

My publisher, Tony, for giving a home to Carmine and Louve and making this book a reality.

My editor, Katarina, for pushing me to make this story shine. You are truly the best.

My friends Lorène and Yawen, for always being here to support my writing and harass me about signed copies.

My mother, Patricia, for always cheering me up and believing in my writing, even if she can't read my stories. (I promise I'll get them translated into French.)

The Books Inc. Mountain View Writers' Meet-Up folks, also known as the Book Inkers, for being supportive, kind, and simply amazing people. (I'm glad we finally have a shorter name!)

And you, for reading this book. You are the reason I keep sitting in front of my computer every day to write stories. Thank you!

About the Author

Millie Abecassis is a writer of speculative fiction from France. She is a graduate of the Panthéon-Sorbonne University and now works in the biotech industry. *Daughters of the Blue Moon* is her debut novella. She is the founder of #SmallPitch and the co-founder of the Small Spec Book Awards. Millie lives in San Jose, California with her husband and their cats. You can learn more about her writing and other endeavors at www.millieabecassis.com. (Photo: Clayton J. Mitchell)